WEATHER OR NOT

Also by Sarah Mlynowski, Lauren Myracle,
& Emily Jenkins:

UPSIDE ★ DOWN MAGIC

WEATHER OR NOT

by

Sarah
MLYNOWSKI,

Lauren
MYRACLE,

and

Emily
JENKINS

SCHOLASTIC INC.

To Lauren Walters and Deb Shapiro, because we are grateful for all their magic.

Copyright © 2018 by Sarah Mlynowski, Lauren Myracle, and Emily Jenkins

This book was originally published in hardcover by Scholastic Press in 2018.

All rights reserved. Published by Scholastic Inc., *Publishers since 1920.* SCHOLASTIC and associated logos are trademarks and/or registered trademarks of Scholastic Inc.

The publisher does not have any control over and does not assume any responsibility for author or third-party websites or their content.

No part of this publication may be reproduced, stored in a retrieval system, or transmitted in any form or by any means, electronic, mechanical, photocopying, recording, or otherwise, without written permission of the publisher. For information regarding permission, write to Scholastic Inc., Attention: Permissions Department, 557 Broadway, New York, NY 10012.

ISBN 978-1-338-22148-0

10 9 8 7 6 5 4 3 2   20 21 22 23

Printed in the U.S.A.   40
This edition first printing 2019

Book design by Abby Dening

op. Pop. Boom!

Totally by accident, Nory Horace turned into a squid-puppy.

In other words, a squippy. When it happened, she dropped her backpack. And her lunch bag. In her squippy form, she couldn't hold on to them. *Zamboozle!* she thought. *Bad timing.*

Before fluxing into the squippy, Nory had been waiting outside her classroom at Dunwiddle Magic School.

Waiting.

And stressing.

Alone in the hallway.

The other students had all gone home or to after-school programs. Nory was still here because she was waiting for her parent-teacher conference.

Nory's teacher was Ms. Starr, and Nory's parent-person was Aunt Margo.

Aunt Margo was late.

Ms. Starr was late, too. At the end of the school day, Nory had watched her shrug into a bright yellow cardigan and pin one of her braids back into her bun before saying that she was running down to the store for some chocolate.

Ms. Starr ate chocolate? Nory had never imagined teachers eating chocolate. She always pictured them eating vegetables.

Nory's father ate lots of vegetables and he was a teacher. In fact, he was the headmaster of a fancy private magic school called Sage Academy. Nory's older brother and sister went to Sage . . . but Nory didn't. She had flunked the entrance exam.

It had been a terrible day. During the Big Test, Nory's magic went wonky. She had fluxed into several mixed-up animals. Also, she had totally forgotten to hold on to her human mind, the way she was supposed to when she changed into animal form. She might have bitten someone.

Okay, she *had* bitten someone.

It was too awful to remember.

After she flunked the Big Test, Father sent Nory to live with Aunt Margo in the town of Dunwiddle. Here, Nory could go to an Upside-Down Magic class and learn to work her unusual magic.

At Dunwiddle Magic School, Nory worked hard. She studied magic, math, science, literature, and social studies. She grew to love Ms. Starr. She was even starting to love having upside-down magic.

But in Ms. Starr's Upside-Down Magic class, it was difficult to know if she was doing things *right*.

Ms. Starr taught headstands, hula-hooping, and poetry recital. The students learned to calm their minds and express their creative spirits. They even painted with their feet.

How was Nory supposed to know if she was doing good work?

What *was* good foot painting, anyway?

Nory could be failing and not even know it.

She checked the clock on the wall. It was 3:06. The parent-teacher conference was supposed to have started at 3:00.

Now it was 3:07.

AHHHH!

Where were Aunt Margo and Ms. Starr? It was very stressful!

That's why Nory Horace turned into a squippy. *Pop. Pop. Boom!* Squippy-Nory had a golden retriever head and golden retriever front legs, with squid tentacles at the back.

Oh, drat-doodles, she thought. *Not now!*

Typical Fluxers turned themselves into typical animals, like kittens. When they got stronger, they learned to transform into dogs, goats, gerbils, and hamsters. But since Nory was an Upside-Down Fluxer, she fluxed into mixed-up animals. She was learning to control her magic and was getting pretty good at holding the shape of just plain kitten. But when she started off as something un-kitten? Like a puppy? She had a *very* hard time holding on to her human mind.

Squippy-Nory looked at the empty hallway.

Run! Play! thought Squippy-Nory.

No! Girl-Nory told herself. *Sit down. Flux back to human form! Parent-teacher conference is about to start!*

Yum yum yum, smell all the yummy smells! thought Squippy-Nory.

Her dog paws skittered down the hall, dragging her squid tentacles behind her.

What's in that locker? wondered Squippy-Nory. *Stinky, sweaty gym shoe smell—mine, mine, mine!*

Squippy-Nory nosed the locker's metal slats. She got it open.

Books, papers, and pencils spilled out. Stinky sneakers spilled out!

Yip-yip-yooray!

Nom nom, slobber slobber.

Squippy-Nory took a sneaker in her mouth and hurtled farther down the hall.

Ooooh, paper bag! Lying there with nobody around! Smells like tuna sandwich.

Flinging aside the shoe, Squippy-Nory attacked the bag. It ripped open—*zwoop!*

Where was the tuna? All she could find was an empty bit of plastic wrap. Squippy-Nory grabbed the paper bag with strong puppy teeth.

R-r-ruff! Tear, rip, shred!

"Nory?" A voice spoke from above.

Squippy-Nory froze.

Surprise! Embarrassment! Stress about the conference!

Nory couldn't help it. She did what squids do when they get nervous.

She squirted ink. On the floor.

Aunt Margo was standing with her hands on her hips. She wore sneakers, jeans, and a puffy coat. Her pale cheeks were pink from the cold November air, and her short hair was covered by a knitted cap.

"Nory, I know that's you," she said. "Can you flux back now, please?"

Sloop-slither-pop! Nory was human again, sitting on her bottom in the hall. A quick body scan told her that, yep, she was back to her full girl-self: smallish in size, brown skin, big hair, rainbow sweater, and three plastic rings she'd gotten from a vending machine at the corner store. Her pants were dry, thank goodness. But next to her was a medium-sized puddle of ink.

Nory scrambled to her feet. "I might have fluxed into a squippy."

"Yes, I saw," said Aunt Margo. She surveyed the mess. There was a smile at the corner of her mouth. "So did you piddle on the hall . . . or squiddle?"

Nory winced. "It's squid ink."

Aunt Margo laughed. She strode to the bathroom and returned with paper towels. She mopped up the squiddle, threw the lunch bag in the trash, and put the shoes and school supplies back in the locker. Then she squirted hand sanitizer on her hands.

"Ready for the conference?" Aunt Margo asked as they walked to Ms. Starr's room.

Nory wasn't ready at all—but she squared her shoulders and nodded.

2

When Nory was little, she didn't have magic powers. Nobody did. Powers came in when people turned ten. So for preschool through fourth grade, kids went to ordinary school. Then, when their talents bubbled up, they started fifth grade at magic school.

There were five types of typical magic. Schools put students into classes based on those types.

Fuzzies communicated with animals. They learned how to direct schools of fish or send birds on errands.

Flares had fire magic. They studied heat and flames, from cooking to rocket launching.

Flyers practiced height, speed, and direction. Really powerful Flyers like Aunt Margo could take passengers. Others could make objects elevate.

Flickers had invisibility magic. Some learned to make things disappear. Others learned to make *themselves* vanish.

Finally, Fluxers could transform into animals. They learned to refine their animal bodies down to the last whisker. They practiced holding on to their human minds.

People whose magic didn't fit neatly into one of these typical five Fs were said to have upside-down magic. That was the nice way to put it.

When Nory and Aunt Margo walked into the UDM classroom for their conference, Ms. Starr was eating from a bag of choco fire trucks on her desk. "Would you like some chocolate?" she asked. Then she and Aunt Margo shook hands and said adult things while Nory unwrapped a fire truck and ate it.

Ms. Starr walked Aunt Margo around the classroom, showing her poems pinned to bulletin boards, the collection of cheery umbrellas in the corner in case of indoor rain, maps the students had made, and reports they'd written on unicorns.

Nory was nervous. She sat at a table and folded the empty fire-truck wrapper into fourths.

Then she unfolded it and flattened it out.

Then she looked up. Ooh! Ms. Starr was taking a rabbit out of a box! It had to be her companion bunny, whom Nory had heard about but never officially met!

"This is Carrot," Ms. Starr said to Aunt Margo. "She's a Miniature Cashmere Lop, and she's been working with Nory's friend Pepper. My magic talent allows her to communicate in English when we're under the same roof." Ms. Starr patted the bunny's soft back. "Carrot will be coming to school regularly from now on."

Ms. Starr had upside-down magic just like her students. She was an Upside-Down Fuzzy who could make animals actually *talk* people language.

The bunny spoke. "I get bored while Eloise is at work," she explained as Ms. Starr put her gently on the desk. "And I like the salad bar in the cafeteria. Nice to meet you, Nory and Margo."

Wow. Nory had heard about Carrot from Pepper, but she had never met a talking animal.

Aunt Margo held out her hand, and the bunny touched it gently with her paw. Nory did the same.

"You can pet me if you'd like," said Carrot.

Nory patted the bunny. The fur was dense and soft.

"And you can scratch my ears, if you're so inclined," Carrot continued. "But my tummy is off-limits."

Nory scratched Carrot's ears. They were like velvet.

Meanwhile, Ms. Starr pulled out a folder that said *Elinor Boxwood Horace* on it. "I have your report card right here."

Oh. Right. Nory's heart began to pound.

Would her grades be okay?

She knew she'd worked hard, but then, she'd always worked hard before, and she'd always disappointed Father.

With Father, a P on a report card was not acceptable. P stood for *Proficient*.

A lot of parents were happy when their kids got Ps. But Father wanted all Os, for *Outstanding*.

In ordinary school, Nory had earned Ps and Os, but she'd also had a few Qs—for *Quite good, but nothing to bang a drum about*—in science. And occasionally she'd had Rs in classroom behavior. R stood for *Regrettable*.

Father had scolded her about the Qs and Rs. And he had shaken his head at the Ps, too.

"Don't be scared," said Margo, squeezing Nory's shoulder. "Whatever your grades are, they're just a chance to learn how well your work is paying off. Then you can ask for help, or try a different approach, if you need it."

"Or you can just celebrate," said Ms. Starr, handing the report card to Nory.

O for literature.

O for math.

O for science.

O for social studies.

O for gym.

O for art.

O for magic.

Nory was a straight-O student!

"Zamboozle!" Nory grinned.

"You earned every one of those Os, Nory," said Ms. Starr.

Aunt Margo swooped her into a hug. "I'm over-joyed," she said. "So impressed."

Overjoyed, Nory repeated inside her head. *Another O!*

"Knock, knock!" It was Coach Vitomin, sticking his bald head into the classroom.

"Coach!" Ms. Starr exclaimed. "Come on in."

Coach bounded in and shook Aunt Margo's hand vigorously. "Fantastic to see you," he boomed.

"Ms. Starr asked me to drop by to discuss Nory's tutoring progress. How about a demonstration, hmm?"

Coach Vitomin was Nory's fluxing tutor. He had helped her learn strategies to manage her magic. And yeah, today's squippy adventure proved that she still didn't have complete control, but she *was* getting stronger.

"Kitten!" Coach commanded now.

*Remember, you are a straight-*O *student,* Nory thought. *Just breathe and focus. Keep your human mind. You've got this.*

Stretch-pop! She fluxed into a solid black kitten. A *perfect* solid black kitten.

"Look how cute she is!" Aunt Margo exclaimed proudly. She hadn't seen Nory's kitten for a while.

"She has all the details she's supposed to have," said Coach. "Whiskers, yellow eyes, the length of the tail. A lot of beginner students have trouble getting more than a stubby tail."

Kitten-Nory flicked her nice long tail.

"Now let's see some sports skills," said Coach. "Heads up!" He tossed a ball of yarn. Kitten-Nory leapt into the air and batted it. Coach caught it and threw it back.

Kitten-Nory spiked and tail-whacked, showing off the skills she had learned at her after-school kittenball club.

"When school started," Coach told Aunt Margo, "Nory couldn't hold any animal form. Now she keeps her kitten shape for at least fifteen minutes."

"Can we see a dritten, please?" asked Ms. Starr.

Kitten-Nory readied herself, tail quivering. It was much harder to hold on to her human mind when she did mixed-up animals. Learning to do so was a big part of her UDM studies.

"Go on," said Coach. "Show the dritten."

Kitten-Nory felt her jaw muscles flex. Her teeth grew pointed. Her claws became large and powerful. She had the exquisite sensation of sprouting wings. They were powerful, shimmering dragon wings. She flapped them and launched into the air, flying gently around the room.

A rippling sensation fizzed in her belly, and she roared—but not *too* loudly. Red-and-orange flames licked the air.

"Great controlled fire breath!" Ms. Starr marveled.

"Nory, please land and chase your tail," Coach instructed. He kept his tone level, but Dritten-Nory knew he was nervous. As a kitten, chasing her tail was no big deal. It was play. But dragon teeth were made for fighting. She really had to keep her human mind and not get overexcited.

Don't rip your own tail off, Dritten-Nory told herself.

She landed. She swiveled her head and spotted her kitten tail. Her furry, fluffy tail. It swished and seemed to say, *You can't get me, ha-ha!*

Dritten-Nory lunged for her tail. Round and round she chased it until she caught its end with her sharp teeth.

Attack! Attack!

Aunt Margo gasped. "She'll hurt herself!"

"That's too rough, Nory. Drop it," Coach said sternly.

Dritten-Nory didn't want to drop it! *The tail was furry! It was alive! Arggggggghhhhhh! Kill! Kill!*

But the girl part of Nory heard Coach's command. Also, her tail kind of hurt.

Drop it, she told herself. *That's your own tail! Zamboozle! Keep hold of your human mind! This is your parent-teacher conference!*

She dropped it.

Then she forced herself to sit down neatly with her front paws right next to each other. "Meow."

"Well done," Coach said, relief flooding his voice. "Flux back, please."

Swish-crunch! She was Nory again. Girl-Nory, who as a dritten *had chased her tail and not eaten it.* Hooray!

"I'd say that concludes our conference," Ms. Starr said. "Unless either of you have questions?"

Aunt Margo asked something about the curriculum. It was boring, and instead of paying attention, Nory ate another fire truck and glowed.

She, Elinor Boxwood Horace, had a perfect report card. Father would be proud.

3

Willa Ingeborg heard cheering inside Ms. Starr's room.

She wanted to peek in, but she worried she'd be spotted. Instead, she slumped in one of the chairs Ms. Starr had set out in the hall. She crossed her arms over her chest and tried to avoid eye contact with her parents.

Who was in there?

It sounded like they were having fun. But why?

Parent-teacher conferences weren't fun. Parent-teacher conferences were the opposite of fun.

Willa didn't want to hear how she wasn't "fulfilling her potential." She'd heard it every year in ordinary school.

Every.

Single.

Year.

"Willa, sit up straight, please," her mother said.

Willa's mother sat on one side of her. Her father was on the other. Both her parents were six feet tall and blond. They looked like statues. Willa's sister was the same.

Not Willa. Willa was short and looked more like an elf than a work of art.

More happy sounds from inside. Were they having a *party* in there?

Maybe it was Elliott's conference. His family was very jolly. Elliott was an Upside-Down Flare. That meant he flared very weakly, but he could also freeze things instead of setting them on fire. His parents thought it was cool. He could make slushies out of plain lemonade.

Willa was an Upside-Down Flare, too, but her magic was more problematic. Her parents didn't think it was cool at all.

Well, they didn't come out and say that. But it was true.

Her father, Chase Ingeborg, was a Fluxer and a scientist. He spent a week each month in South America, fluxing into lizards to help other scientists study lizards in their natural habitat. Last year he was on the cover of *Fluxing Science* magazine.

Willa's mother, Gaia, was a Fluxer, too. She worked from home doing watercolor paintings for greeting cards. When she needed to relax, she fluxed into a house cat and took naps in patches of sun.

If Willa had been a typical Flare, like her sister, Edith, everything would have been fine.

If she had been a cool Upside-Down Flare, like Elliott, it would have been fine, too. Slushies for everyone!

But no.

Willa Ingeborg made it rain. Indoors.

Only indoors.

She rained when she was scared. She rained when she was nervous. She rained when she was startled, and when she grew sad or angry. She rained without meaning to, and she couldn't always turn it off.

Until Willa's magic had bubbled up at the age of ten, Willa's mother had spent part of every day fluxed into a house cat. But cats hate getting wet, so now Willa's mother fluxed only outdoors—or when Willa wasn't nearby.

Willa's mother struggled with Willa's magic in other ways, too. Willa's rain had ruined many of her paintings. It had spoiled the carpets. And the couches. And the mattresses.

No matter how many times the family tackled the house with bleach and cleaning products, their home still smelled of damp and mold.

"Chase, I really do need to get back to my studio," Willa's mother said now as they waited in the hall. "I have an appointment at four fifteen. Would you please see what's holding things up?"

Willa's father fluxed immediately into a tiny lizard. He skittered over and crept underneath the door of Ms. Starr's classroom. After a minute, he popped back out and turned into a human again. "There's a cat with *wings* in there," he said to Willa's mother. "Wonkiest fluxing I've ever seen!"

"Don't say *wonkiest*," chided Gaia. "Remember the UDM handout Ms. Starr sent home? She wants us to say *different* or *unusual*. Not *wonky*."

"*Different* is certainly one way of putting it," Willa's father said. He shook his head. "A cat! With *wings*! When it opened its mouth, I saw flames shoot out!"

"My goodness, I don't like the sound of that," Willa's mother fretted. "Why is everybody sounding so cheerful, then? Are they *laughing* at that poor child—a child who can't even manage a proper cat?"

"Her name's Nory," Willa said, knowing what her father had seen. "She turns into a dritten."

"Dritten?" said her mother.

"Kitten plus dragon," explained Willa. "She fluxes into a dritten on purpose, actually. She's getting really good."

Just then, Nory (in human form) flung open the classroom door. She strode into the hall, followed by Coach, Ms. Starr, and Nory's aunt Margo.

"Willa!" Nory cried, putting her hands on Willa's shoulders and bouncing up and down. "Are you up next? Guess what? Ms. Starr brought her bunny! Do you like bunnies? Of course you like bunnies. And Carrot is, like, the smartest bunny in the world. She *talks*! Omigosh. Best conference *ever*!"

"Um, these are my parents," Willa said.

Nory put on her parent face, straightened her spine, and shook hands. "Hello, I'm Elinor Horace. Nice to meet you."

Ms. Starr smiled brightly at the Ingeborgs. "Come in, come in!"

Willa waved good-bye to Nory and followed her parents into the classroom. Inside, Ms. Starr took a seat. She gestured at the chairs arranged in a semi-circle in front of her. "Make yourselves comfortable!"

Willa glanced around the room. "Where's the bunny?"

Ms. Starr winked. "Carrot, sweetheart," she called. "Hop on out and meet Willa!"

"Sleeping," came a crotchety voice from behind the desk. "It's past my nap time."

Willa craned her neck. She couldn't see the bunny.

"She's persnickety," Ms. Starr said, waving her hand through the air. "You'll meet her another time."

"When I'm not *sleeping*," Carrot called. Willa decided Carrot must be cozied into one of Ms. Starr's desk drawers. Ms. Starr shrugged and looked at Willa's parents like, *Rabbits! What can you do?*

Willa was disappointed. Carrot had talked to Nory. Why not Willa?

"Well, Mr. and Ms. Ingeborg, I am delighted to chat with you," Ms. Starr said, offering them choco fire trucks.

Willa's mother handed one to Willa but didn't eat one herself. She leaned forward. "We do hope this class has helped our daughter," Gaia said. "She has such potential. But Chase and I both worry that—"

"Has she made progress?" Willa's father asked flatly. "That's what we're here to discuss, isn't it?"

"Willa is a joy to have in the classroom," said Ms. Starr. "But we *are* having some challenges." She grabbed a folder with Willa's name on it and handed it to the Ingeborgs.

"In terms of academic subjects, Willa is very capable of mastering the material. She's quite musical. At memorizing poetry, she's at the top of the class. Math, literature, social studies—if she applied herself, she could excel at every one of these subjects."

"She isn't applying herself?" her father asked.

"She could work harder," Ms. Starr admitted.

Gaia pursed her lips. Chase frowned.

"But that's a simple issue, easily solved," continued Ms. Starr. She looked at Willa. "We can brainstorm some study habits that might help you. What I'd really like to discuss is her magical talent. You have a remarkable daughter, Mr. and Ms. Ingeborg. You should be very proud."

Willa's mother nodded cautiously.

"I'm sure you have noticed that Willa becomes anxious in social situations," Ms. Starr continued.

Willa's cheeks burned. Of course she was anxious! Wouldn't anyone be anxious, knowing that at any moment, for any reason, you might *rain* all over everyone?

"I think her anxiety is connected to her struggle to control her magic," Ms. Starr went on. She shifted her gaze to Willa. "I want to help you with this, Willa."

Ms. Starr turned back to Willa's parents. "She's well liked by her classmates. She's a kind and loyal friend. She has strong connections to Marigold and Elliott in particular."

Willa's mom was looking at the report card. "She has mostly Qs. She has a Regrettable in gym and a Proficient in literature."

"Proficient?" Willa's dad asked. "Didn't you say she was top of the class? Why isn't she getting an Outstanding?"

"Willa *is* at the top of the class when it comes to memorizing," said Ms. Starr. "But memorization is only one of the skills we work on. Willa wrote the first three-quarters of a lovely essay on 'Mermaids of the Kelpy Forest,' but she stopped midway through. She never wrote the conclusion."

It was true. Willa hadn't finished her essay, even though she had liked "Mermaids of the Kelpy Forest" and could recite it by heart.

It was also true that she hadn't done all her math homework.

Or even very much of her math homework.

She had let Marigold write up the science labs when they were partners.

And she had never memorized the things she was supposed to for the social studies test because, honestly, it was really boring.

She liked gym, but often forgot to bring her sneakers. She liked art, but had lost her portfolio a couple of times. She liked Ms. Starr's magic studies, and she liked her tutoring sessions with Elliott and Ms. Cruciferous, but she didn't feel like she was making good progress. Yes, she could now make rhythms with raindrops over small bowls, and could form tiny rainstorms over people's heads—but the hard truth was, she continued to soak the UDM classroom at least once a day.

There was a bin of umbrellas in the corner because of Willa's rain. In fact, the Ingeborgs had just donated nine new ones in bright colors, because the yellow ones from the start of the school year were bent and broken from so much use.

There was no rug in the rug area, because of Willa's rain.

People's projects had been ruined.

People's clothes were always wet.

It was depressing for everyone. Especially Willa.

"Willa, sweetie, I can tell by your face that I'm making you sad," Ms. Starr said kindly. "That's not my goal. I believe in you. You know that, right?"

An enormous soggy rain cloud pressed down on top of Willa. That's what it felt like. She had a lump in her throat that she knew too well. She was going to cry.

Do not cry, she told herself. *Don't do it! Stop!*

A small raindrop hit the garbage can with a plink.

4

P lease!" her mother snapped. "Not now!"

"I can't help it," Willa whispered.

Her rain was coming down hard and spreading out to soak more and more of the classroom. Ms. Starr grabbed three umbrellas. She opened one for herself and handed the other two to Willa's parents.

"Thank you," Willa's dad said, holding his umbrella high. Willa ducked under it with him as the rain poured.

"Eloise!" came a voice from Ms. Starr's desk. A rust-colored bunny with sleepy, grumpy eyes peered at the group from over the edge of the desk. She was sopping wet.

Ms. Starr ran to the rabbit and scooped her up.

"I'm sorry!" wailed Willa. Tears dripped down her cheeks.

Ms. Starr placed the rabbit gently in an empty cupboard where it was dry.

"Just relax, Willa," ordered Willa's father. "Do your mental exercises or whatever."

"Calm down," her mother said.

Willa hated being told to calm down.

She felt what she felt! She couldn't just change it! The rain came down harder. Puddles formed on the floor.

"Why don't the three of us finish our discussion in another room?" Ms. Starr said to Willa's parents. "Willa, stay here for a minute so the rain doesn't move outside the classroom. Try your centering exercises, like reciting 'Mermaids of the Kelpy Forest.' Or do a headstand. Maybe you want to try the deep-breathing exercises."

Water poured down the back of Willa's shirt, into her shoes, and down her face. Ms. Starr and Willa's parents left her alone in the classroom.

Worst. Parent-teacher conference. Ever.

Willa was in a headstand when she heard the classroom door creak open. Elliott Cohen's sneakered feet walked over, protected by an umbrella. He was a thin boy, pale and tall, with hair that sprung in loopy curls all over his head.

"Did Ms. Starr send you in?" asked Willa, still upside down.

"She didn't *send* me," said Elliott. "I thought I could help. My family has the next conference."

Willa flipped out of her headstand and stood up. Strands of sopping hair clung to her face. She pushed them away.

"My parent-teacher conference was bad," she told him. "I knew my report card wouldn't be perfect, but it was worse than I thought."

"Come under the umbrella," said Elliott.

Willa joined him, and he gave her the handle. Then he opened his palms, stepped out into the storm, and . . . the rain turned to snow. Puffy snowflakes swirled across the ceiling. The snow was colder than the rain, and would still damage the furniture, but it was beautiful. And calm. Happy, instead of sad and angry.

Snowing was something Elliott and Willa had learned to do in tutoring, as a pair. Willa made the rain. Elliott froze it just as it began to fall.

They watched the snow cover the desks.

"Let's do the deep-breathing thing," said Elliott.

"I hate the deep-breathing thing," said Willa.

"It's hokey, I know. But it does kind of work."

"Okay, fine."

They breathed deep breaths as the snow fell. Then Willa recited three poems.

Then they deep-breathed some more, and the snow finally stopped.

The classroom was white. They were shivering.

But Willa's storm had passed.

• • •

After changing into dry clothes, Willa and Elliott found the janitor and told her about the snowstorm in Ms. Starr's classroom. The janitor said not to worry, and that she'd take care of it. Willa's spirits lifted.

When they returned to their classroom, though, Nory was still in the hall. Her aunt was cheerfully chatting with Elliott's parents. Ms. Starr and the Ingeborgs were nowhere to be found.

Drat.

Willa *did* like Nory. Usually. Nory was friendly and always looked on the bright side. She had good ideas and a big heart, and she wore fun clothes.

But: Nory talked *a lot*. And she was a bit of a show-off.

And Nory was Elliott's best friend. He always went off with her.

"Nory!" he called. "Since Ms. Starr's not here, let's see if the library's open."

"The library?" Nory wrinkled her brow. "Why?"

"I found a book about Blurper Dragons! Come see!"

"Oh! Because Blurper Dragon is the kind of dragon I flux into!" cried Nory.

Sheesh, thought Willa. Ever since their class had been on that field trip to the dragon rescue center, Nory jumped at any chance to talk about Blurper Dragons. But Nory *didn't* flux into a dragon, not technically. She only fluxed into a kitten and then added *bits* of Blurper Dragon to make the dritten.

"That's why I want to show you the book!" Elliott said.

He took off running, toward the library. Nory followed.

Willa leaned, forgotten, against the wall. She listened to Margo and the Cohens talk about the school fund-raiser until her parents came to collect her.

5

The next morning, Nory ate breakfast alone. Aunt Margo had left early to fly a taxi client.

Nory didn't mind. She played loud music on the radio. She put on her striped leggings and the dress with the owls on it. She poured herself a bowl of Fruity Doodles, ate them quickly, and ran out the door when Elliott rang the buzzer, like he always did.

She had stayed up late reading the Blurper Dragon book. "Hey, listen to this," she said as they walked to school. "Blurper Dragons *love* fruit! And guess who else loves fruit. Guess guess guess!"

"Is this a trick question?" Elliott asked.

"Me!" Nory cried. "*I* love fruit, too!"

"You don't say."

"I *do* say. I am all about fruit. I had fruit-flavored cereal for breakfast, and I have plans to eat an orange at lunchtime."

The day felt sparkly and bright. Ahead, they saw their friend Andres Padillo high in the air. His sister, Carmen, held his leash. Andres was an Upside-Down Flyer who couldn't come down from the sky. Whenever he was outdoors, he had to be on a leash or wear a backpack full of bricks.

"It's a good morning, right, Andres?" Nory called, waving. Andres waved back. Nory turned to Elliott. "So. How was your parent-teacher conference?"

"Medium good," he answered. "My tutor couldn't be there, but I got an O in magic and Ms. Starr said a lot of stuff about me being a good community member that made my dad all proud. My grades aren't perfect—but good enough that my parents are happy. We ended up meeting in Coach Vitomin's office while the janitor dried out the UDM classroom. That place smells like seaweed snacks."

"It totally does," Nory agreed. "Did you go back in the UDM classroom? Were the sculptures safe in the cupboard? Or did Willa soak them again?" Three days ago, Willa had drenched Nory's clay Blurper Dragon sculpture. Everyone's sculptures had been ruined, in fact. Willa had gotten frustrated in math class, and then—whoosh—rain everywhere. They'd had to start their projects over and hide the drying sculptures in a cupboard. All their papers were always stored safely in plastic boxes in their desks.

"The sculptures were fine. She can't help raining," Elliott said.

"I know," Nory said. "I just wish she wasn't such a crybaby. Every time she gets upset, the whole class has to suffer."

Elliott stopped walking. "Whoa."

"What?"

"You shouldn't call her a crybaby," he said. "Labels like that are pretty mean."

Nory's face heated up. She knew he was right. She hadn't meant to be mean; it had just slipped out.

"I'm sorry," she said. "I won't say that again."

Neither of them spoke for a minute. They resumed walking.

"Did you get to meet Carrot?" she asked, finally, to change the subject.

"Carrot is the best," Elliott said. "So fluffy! I got to see Ms. Starr blow her dry with a hair dryer."

They linked arms, laughing, and chatted the rest of the way to school.

In Ms. Starr's class, the students started the day with headstands. Nothing new, but it was fun. Nory was *crushing* her headstand. She could hold it for two minutes easily. It made her feel strong. Ms. Starr said that learning the control it took to hold a headstand would help her learn to manage her fluxing. Plus a headstand changed the way a person saw things: What was upside down? What was right side up?

Then the students did interpretive dance. Ms. Starr put on music and encouraged them to get in touch with their emotions through movement. The idea was that art and magic were both related to feelings. If you expressed your feelings in art, they wouldn't build up and overwhelm you in magical ways.

No one much liked interpretive dance. Marigold Ramos, who had unusual shrinking magic, said it wouldn't be so bad if Ms. Starr let them dance to pop songs. (No one had been able to put a label on Marigold's magic. She wasn't an Upside-Down Fluxer, Fuzzy, Flare, Flicker, *or* Flyer. She just shrank things and couldn't make them big again.)

Nory's friend Bax Kapoor said it was embarrassing no matter what they danced to. Bax was an Upside-Down Fluxer like Nory. But he fluxed into objects, never animals.

Today, just when the music started, Bax turned into a piano. Had he done it to avoid dancing? Possibly.

Still, his piano looked really good! And Nory could tell that Bax still had his human mind in his piano shape. He played "Crazy-Daisy Shame," one of her favorite songs.

Don't don't don't
It's a crazy-daisy shame
Don't keep your honey bunch
Out in the rain!

It was amazing, watching the keys move up and down on their own. The class danced to "Crazy-Daisy Shame" instead of the boring classical symphony Ms. Starr had been playing through the speakers. It was much more fun than usual.

When the song was over, Ms. Starr told Piano-Bax she was happy to see his progress. She assigned Elliott to wheel him to the medical office. Bax still couldn't turn back into his human form without help from the school nurse.

Later, after Bax and Elliott returned, it was time for social studies. "For the next week and a half," Ms. Starr explained, "we will take a break from studying government and focus instead on the history of our very own town of Dunwiddle. Can anyone tell us why?"

Most of the kids put their hands up, but Nory didn't have a clue. Why did everyone know the answer?

She looked around. Bax didn't know either, she could tell. And neither did Marigold.

Oh! Nory realized: Everyone with their hand in the air had grown up here in Dunwiddle.

Pepper Phan, an Upside-Down Fuzzy who terrified animals.

Sebastian Boondoggle, an Upside-Down Flicker who could see invisible things.

Also, Elliott, Andres, and Willa.

Nory, Bax, and Marigold didn't know the answer because they had all moved to town specifically for the Upside-Down Magic class.

"Yes, Pepper?" Ms. Starr said. "Why, as winter approaches, is it a special time for our town?"

"Because of Bing Day on November sixteenth," Pepper said.

"That's exactly right," Ms. Starr said.

"*Bing* Day?" Marigold blurted.

"What's Bing Day?" Nory asked.

"Bing Day is the most important holiday of the year for Dunwiddle," explained Ms. Starr. She pulled down the projection screen and fiddled with the laptop on her desk. A video began. The title credits read: *Bing Day—Bravo for Our Best and Brightest!*

"This again?" complained Sebastian. He was the one who saw invisible things. Not every single invisible thing, but lots of them. Like sound waves. Right now, Sebastian had on a pair of large, dark aviator-style goggles. The goggles blocked his sight on the sides and helped reduce the chaos of the visible sounds. "Every single teacher makes us watch this, every single year," he said.

Elliott groaned and put his head down on his desk. Pepper did the same. But Nory was curious.

The video was narrated by a man whose voice rumbled like a freight train. He explained that in the olden days, female Flares worked mainly as maids and cooks. Back then, other Flare jobs were only open to men.

"What? That's crazy cakes!" Nory huffed.

"Shhh. Listen," said Ms. Starr.

The film flashed to a clip of a middle-aged woman with tiny, round glasses and brown skin. She wore a tweedy jacket and a long skirt. Her name was Zeponiah Bing, Nory learned, and she was born and raised in the town of Dunwiddle. She was a Flare, but she had no interest in working as a maid or a cook. Instead, Bing went to an all-women's college. While there, she developed her naturally strong Flare magic beyond what anyone had expected of her. She became able to heat extremely large areas to very precise temperatures. She graduated at the top of her class and went on to become a famous professor of

Flare Studies at a fancy college, one of the only female teachers there.

During the famously long winter of 1893, the town of Dunwiddle was buried in snow. There was a shortage of food. People died. When Professor Bing learned of the crisis, she immediately and heroically returned to her hometown and used her remarkable heating magic to thaw the land without damaging buildings or crops.

She saved lives! She was awesome!

"For these reasons and many more, Dunwiddle celebrates Professor Bing's birthday every year with a magnificent parade," the narrator said as clips of past parades showed people wearing costumes from olden times.

"And for you young people, here's a fun fact," he continued. Nory's classmates stirred, and to her surprise, all of those who'd grown up in Dunwiddle recited the fact along with him. "It has never, ever rained on Bing Day!"

The video ended with the idea that maybe Professor Bing's unusually strong Flare magic was connected to the power of the sun. Some people believed that was why the sun always shone on her special day, the day of the parade. "Nonbelievers can roll their eyes all they want," a young woman said fervently into the camera. "But this is magic, people. Sun magic. Bing magic!"

Ms. Starr turned off the film. Nory blinked.

"Fascinating, isn't it?" Ms. Starr said.

"Do you believe in it?" asked Nory. "Bing magic?" She thought about how much was unknown when it came to magic.

Ms. Starr didn't answer the question. Instead, she said, "This year, all the fifth graders will make a poster about some aspect of Bing Day history. You will work in pairs. Each pair will be expected to draw on at least five different sources to make history come alive!"

Sighs and moans rippled through the room.

"I'm asleep already," said Andres from the ceiling.

"We have to do something like this every year," Sebastian explained to Nory, Bax, and Marigold. "It's terribly repetitive."

"Then I suggest you find a way to make it *not* repetitive," Ms. Starr said tartly. "Boredom is a failure of the imagination. Our posters will be on display all through the halls of the school on Bing Day. The sixth graders are making dioramas, and the seventh grade will perform the annual Bing Day music concert featuring folk songs of 1893. The eighth grade will treat us to an all-grade read-aloud of 'Zeponiah Bing: An Epic Poem of Praise.'"

"Is she serious?" Marigold whispered to Sebastian.

"She is," said Sebastian.

Ms. Starr went on. "The parade is at four o'clock next Friday."

Nory loved parades. Like, she really, really loved them. "Will there be a marching band?" she asked.

"Yes!" said Ms. Starr. "And antique cars."

Nory bounced on her seat. "What about people on stilts? And Fluxers who flux into really big animals, like rhinos and elephants?"

"To tell the truth—" Ms. Starr began.

"And Flare juggling?!" Nory exclaimed. "Please say there will be Flare juggling! Please!"

Ms. Starr laughed. "I don't actually know. I moved to Dunwiddle for this job. This will be my first Bing Day Parade, too!"

Nory had a genius thought. "We should all wear silly hats," she said. "Everyone in the whole UDM class, to show Bing Day spirit. Maybe antlers?"

"It's not that kind of parade," said Willa.

"It has historical costumes," said Sebastian.

"And we all sing this traditional song," said Andres. "It's kind of *ye olde*."

"What does that even mean?" Bax asked.

"People are in costumes from the 1890s. Bagpipes. Clog dancing."

"Not everyone likes to wear silly hats," added Willa quietly.

"We could still wear antlers," Nory pressed. "Antlers are historical."

Willa gave her a look. "They are not."

"Yes they are!" Nory said. "Antlers came before people, didn't they?"

Willa sighed.

Sheesh, Nory thought. *What's wrong with antlers?*

"I've split you into pairs already, and I'll announce them now so you can start brainstorming your project," said Ms. Starr.

Nory wanted Elliott. Or Pepper. Definitely one or the other.

"Elliott and Bax, you two will work together," Ms. Starr said. "Sebastian is with Marigold, and Andres is with Pepper. Nory and Willa, that leaves the two of you to partner up," Ms. Starr finished. "Sound good? Good. Let the brainstorming begin!"

Boo.

Nory wasn't in the mood to work with Willa. Willa had been rude about Nory's awesome antler idea!

But whatever. They had to. The two of them met at the computer table. Nory brought a pad of paper. And a pen.

Willa brought nothing.

"So what are you interested in?" Nory asked, sitting down.

Willa sat down, too. She picked at her fingernail.

"Women's colleges could be cool," Nory said. "My grandma went to an all-women's college. Or what if we did a poster about sun magic?"

Willa shrugged.

"How about unusual Flares?" Nory tried. "You're an unusual Flare, so that could be interesting!"

"I'm an *Upside-Down* Flare," Willa corrected her.

"That's what I meant," said Nory.

"It's not the same thing." Willa glared at Nory. "Anyway, I'm not interested in Flare Studies."

"Fine," Nory said. "Then what *are* you interested in?"

Willa looked out the window.

"What about weather?" Nory asked.

"What?"

"Weather. Are you interested in weather?"

Willa gave the teeniest of nods.

Nory wrote *WEATHER* on her notepad.

"Okay, so *what* about weather?" Nory pressed. "I guess we could write about snow."

Willa didn't respond.

Sheesh.

Elliott *always* had opinions. Pepper was *always* enthusiastic.

Being partners with Willa was like being partners with a wet, blank notepad.

6

The next afternoon, Willa and Elliott met with their Upside-Down Flare tutor at the high school pool. They entered the large brick building and showed their passes to the guy in the main office. Then they changed in the locker rooms and met again at the pool.

Their tutor was the high school swim coach. Her name was Ms. Cruciferous. She was in her seventies, with olive skin, rosy cheeks, and soft gray hair that she wore loose around her face when it wasn't tucked into a swim cap. She was lean and fit.

Willa had never seen Ms. C in anything other than a swimsuit: sometimes a red tankini, sometimes a one-piece splashed with flowers, sometimes a sporty blue two-piece with racerback straps.

"Willa! Elliott! Fan*tas*tic!" said Ms. C when she saw them. She stopped swimming laps and pulled herself gracefully out of the water. Her suit today was solid black, the top styled like a sports bra. Willa's was her purple tie-dye, because her favorite pink two-piece was in the laundry. Elliott always wore blue trunks.

Ms. Cruciferous was an excellent Flare. She specialized in fireworks and in controlled explosions used for rocket ships or demolishing buildings. At the high school, she taught advanced-level Flares in the pool for safety reasons. After all, in a regular classroom, there were plenty of things a Flare student could set on fire while practicing. Also, the water provided an extra challenge for Flares. They might learn to heat it or flare through it.

For Willa and Elliott, Ms. C taught AquaMerge, a new technique designed to help Upside-Down Flares whose magic connected to water in some way.

"What are we going to do today?" Willa asked.

"Can we do wavemakers?" Elliott asked.

Wavemakers involved blowing softly on the water, making small waves on the surface, then trying to channel magic through the breath to make bigger waves.

"I think we'll do Buckets today," said the teacher. Buckets was an exercise where Ms. C threw buckets of water at Willa and Elliott as they stood in the pool. Elliott was supposed to try to freeze the entire bucket solid before it fell. Willa was supposed to transform the water from a big gush into tiny raindrops. They weren't that good at it yet. It was hard to work quickly under pressure.

"Can we practice snow, too?" asked Willa. The snow she and Elliott had learned to create at the start of the year was the first real progress she had made with her magic.

"Snow makes the pool too cold," said Elliott. "Plus we made snow just the other day. We're always making snow. We don't need to practice it."

"*All* your magic makes the pool cold," Willa teased. "Face up to it."

"Elliott has a point, though," said Ms. C. "We'll do Buckets and then he can work on freezing ice cubes one at a time, getting his aim under control. You and I can work on something else. At the end of the lesson, we can have a free swim and the pool won't be too chilly. Do you want to work on your tiny rain clouds?"

The second big thing Willa had learned in tutoring was to make a miniature, on-purpose rain cloud. She could rain slow or fast from it. If the cloud was super tiny, she could even get the rain to make a rhythm.

"Not really," answered Willa. "Honestly, I want to learn how to stop making enormous gigantic rains without meaning to." She had rained on the classroom twice that day already. Everyone had gotten soaked, and even Ms. Starr had seemed frustrated. "My goal is to never, ever rain by accident."

Ms. C sighed. "I'm sorry," she told Willa. "I simply don't know how to teach you that yet. I'm doing the best I can, but your magic is very unusual. More upside down than Elliott's."

"I just—I really hate it," Willa said. "It upsets everyone. My mom. My friends. It ruins their stuff. And it's so hard to turn off."

Ms. C patted her arm. "Let's work on tiny clouds immediately. We'll skip Buckets for today and see what progress we can make."

While Ms. C set Elliott up with an activity, Willa made a small rain cloud over the pool. It was about the size of a cat.

She made it rain slow. Then fast. Then in a rhythm: *Drip drip DROP drip drip DROP.* When Ms. C rejoined her, the teacher asked Willa to move the rain cloud around. "Put it in the corner over there," she said, pointing.

Willa couldn't.

"What about just moving it a couple of inches?"

Willa couldn't.

"Hm. All right. Try attaching it to something that moves," said the teacher. "Can you attach it to Elliott?"

Willa grinned.

Elliott was sitting on the edge of the pool with an ice-cube tray of water, trying to freeze one cube at a time. He wasn't doing that well. Often he froze two or three cubes at once. Every now and then Ms. C waved her hand at the tray to warm it up again, melting the cubes with her Flare magic so Elliott could start over.

Willa stopped her first cloud and made a new tiny rain cloud appear over Elliott.

"Don't rain on me!" he cried.

"Brawahahahaha!" Willa laughed an evil laugh. "It's an assignment! Ms. Cruciferous wants me to!" Elliott groaned but sat still, being a good sport.

Willa concentrated, and yes, she could attach the cloud to Elliott so it hung right over his head.

It felt like stretching a rubber band from the cloud to his skull. She had done this skill once before, kind of by accident. This time it was definitely on purpose.

"Can I move?" asked Elliott.

Ms. C nodded and Elliott jumped into the pool.

The tiny cloud followed him.

He swam under the water, half a length.

It still followed him.

"No fair!" he sputtered, laughing.

"Can you turn off the rain now, Willa?" said Ms. C. "Make your cloud go away?"

Willa tried.

Nope. It still rained on Elliott.

She tried again.

More nope. It was too hard.

"Can you detach it?" said Ms. C. "Use that Flare technique we worked on, the one where you imagine putting out a match. Touch the tip of your tongue to the roof of your mouth."

Willa did that.

The rain cloud stayed attached to Elliott.

Nothing was working. Willa's heart started to race.

"Recite the mermaid poem!" called Elliott. "That's what Ms. Starr has you do."

"Okay," she said. She forced her eyes closed. She recited the poem quickly at first. The second time she said it, she said it slower. By the third time, she felt calm. After the fourth time, the rain cloud over Elliott disappeared. It felt like forever. But it worked.

"It's definitely harder to turn the rain off when the cloud is attached to something," she said. "Usually I can turn off a tiny one."

"But you *did* move a cloud," said Ms. Cruciferous encouragingly. "And that's more than you've done on purpose before! I think today was some good progress."

They had free swim after that, and Willa and Elliott made the most of it. Willa loved being in the pool. She felt loose and relaxed. She and Elliott splashed each other like maniacs. They did cannonballs in the deep end until it was time for them to go back to school. It was the most fun she'd had all week.

Finally, tired out, they floated on green foam noodles and talked.

"What are you and Nory doing for your Bing Day project?" Elliott asked.

Willa's sense of peace evaporated.

This morning, when Ms. Starr had asked what their project was, Nory had announced they were studying storm patterns related to the Great Frost of 1893. "We'll show how rare it was," Nory had said. "We'll *blah blah blah* and *blah blah blah*, and obviously, we won't forget to *blah blah blah*."

What? Willa hadn't said yes to storm patterns! She wasn't even sure they'd agreed on weather!

"I don't know," Willa told Elliott now. "She's very pushy."

"Sometimes," Elliott admitted. "But she has really interesting ideas."

"Well, her idea this time is boring."

Elliott sighed.

Willa turned her head to look at him. "What?"

Elliott stared at the ceiling. He moved his arms back and forth to keep himself afloat. "I wish you two liked each other. That's all."

"Who said we don't?" Willa stood up in the water, her toes gripping the bottom of the pool. "I like Nory. Does Nory not like me?"

"Of course she likes you."

"Then what? Did she say something about me?"

"She just said . . ." Elliott's voice trailed off.

"That I was stupid?"

"What? No."

"Not paying attention?" she pushed. "Not a team player? What?"

"It wasn't about that at all," Elliott said. "It was . . . you know, she's frustrated because you get so rainy sometimes."

"Did she call me a crybaby?" The word jumped out of Willa's mouth because her sister, Edith, called her a crybaby all the time. She didn't really expect it to be true.

Elliott hesitated.

Willa's throat tightened. "Omigosh, she did! Nory called me a crybaby!"

"She took it back," Elliott rushed to say. "Like, immediately. Labels like that are mean, and she knows it."

"Zowie. She *took it back*. That makes it *so* much better."

"Don't be mad," Elliott said. "She just blurts things out sometimes. And you know she understands about magic getting out of control. It happens to her lots. I didn't mean to tell you. I'm sorry."

Willa flushed.

She *was* a crybaby, and she knew it.

She just didn't know how to keep from being one.

And knowing that people like Nory noticed it— well, that made it so much worse.

7

Nory invited Elliott home after school. They sat in the kitchen of Aunt Margo's small clapboard house, eating turtle-shaped sugar cookies. "We should do homework and get it out of the way," said Elliott after a bit. "I promised my parents I'd try and get my math grade up."

"I have homework from Coach!" Nory told him. She was feeling good about her magic.

"Fluxing homework?" Elliott grinned.

Nory wasn't supposed to flux without adult supervision. No school-age Fluxers were. You had to get a license to flux into certain animals in public. You had to prove that you could hold on to your human mind while in animal form. But Aunt Margo's house wasn't public. And Nory had to practice.

"Kittenball drills!" said Nory. She knew Elliott loved kittenball. "Will you toss the yarn to me? I need to do ten minutes of tail whacks to build up my strength."

Pop pop pop! Nory fluxed into a black kitten and then added some stripes to make a dark gray tabby.

Elliott grinned. "We do have a math test to study for, but I guess it can wait."

Elliott tossed the yarn ball for her, and Nory chased it across the living room and whacked it back. She had kittenball club after school, and she wanted to join the team when she got to seventh grade. They did that for a little while and then Nory stopped for a minute, caught her breath, and fluxed into Dritten-Nory. Her beautiful Blurper-Dragon wings popped from her shoulders, and her claws grew large and scaly. She felt fire breath at the back of her throat, but she didn't let it out.

Elliott tossed the yarn ball again. Dritten-Nory chased it and tail-whacked, flapping her wings sometimes to get to the ball faster. Coach had told her that nothing in the rules said kittens couldn't have dragon features. He hoped having a dritten on the team would give them a chance at the championship.

"Nice!" said Elliott, catching the yarn ball one last time and holding on to it. "The dritten shape is definitely faster than the kitten. And you seem like you kept your human mind!"

Nory turned back into a human. "Yup," she said. "I'm in serious control of my magic." She knew it wasn't totally true. After all, she had squiddled on the floor just a couple of days ago. But it felt good to say it, and maybe saying it would help make it more true. "Unlike you-know-who," she added, sitting down and opening her math folder.

Elliott flushed. "Come on."

"What?"

"Be nice about Willa. She doesn't soak anyone on purpose."

"Three times today! Three! And I know you're friends with her, but she's impossible on the Bing Day project. She doesn't do any work! And she acts like she's not even interested."

Elliott sighed.

"Don't tell her I said this, obviously," Nory added. "Or that I called her a crybaby. I feel bad about that."

Elliott got a blinky, worried look on his face. He tried to smooth it out, and Nory wondered if she had gone too far, but then the phone rang. She picked up. "Hello?"

"Elinor, hello."

Whoa. It was Father.

Father called Nory on Sundays, never in the middle of the week.

"Is everything okay?" she asked.

"Of course!" he said. "Everything is terrific."

"It is?"

"Your aunt sent me a copy of your report card. All Os! That's marvelous!"

Nory lit up. *Marvelous* might be even better than *Outstanding*. Nory reviewed other adjectives Father had used to describe her.

Unruly? Yes.

Disruptive? He used that one often.

Marvelous? Never, ever.

"Thank you," she said, beaming. "I worked really hard."

"I can tell. Keep it up, all right?"

"Yes, Father."

"Excellent. I have to go. I'm still at school. But I wanted to congratulate you on a job well done. I'll call again on Sunday."

"Okay," Nory said. "Thank you, Father. Bye."

"Everything all right?" Elliott asked after she hung up.

Nory nodded, full of wonder. "Better than all right. Everything's marvelous."

• • •

Willa was glad to get home. It had been a tough day.

She knocked on the door to let her mom know she'd arrived, then circled her house to the backyard. Since she only made rain *indoors*, outside was the safest place if she wanted to relax.

Her mother came to greet her, bundled in a warm jacket and carrying her laptop and a thermos of hot chocolate. She and Willa sat side by side on the lawn chairs.

Gaia answered emails while Willa read a book of poetry Ms. Starr had given her. She knew she should study for the math test or work on the stupid Bing project, but she read poem after poem instead. They made her feel . . . well, she couldn't find the right word for it. Poem-y?

Like the world was brighter and the colors more intense.

Like happiness was out there, somewhere.

As the sun began to set, Willa's mother shut her laptop and fluxed into a calico cat. She wasn't a huggy sort of person in her human form, but in cat form, she was affectionate and cuddly. She jumped onto Willa's chair and walked the length of the armrest. Willa held out her hand, and her cat-mother turned around several times and settled in for a nap.

Willa knew that in general, Fluxers felt most at home in their human bodies. It took effort to keep an animal shape, so most Fluxers didn't flux for long. But Willa's mother seemed happiest in her calico form, as if some part of her was actually feline.

Willa read more poems. She even read a few out loud. Before she knew it, the sun had almost disappeared.

"Dinner!" her father called. Cat-Mom yawned and leapt off the chair. She fluxed back into human form.

Indoors, the carpenters who were replacing the living room floor were still at work. Willa wasn't surprised to see them, but she winced at the sound of hammering.

She wished she hadn't ruined the floor.

She wished she hadn't ruined six mattresses since her magic came in, too. Now she, her sister, and her parents had to sleep in hammocks instead of regular beds. Because of her rain, her parents stored the bulk of their possessions in the garden shed. They owned an industrial wet vac to suck up the rainwater that flooded their home so often.

"Are you done with your homework?" her father asked. He placed stir-fried rice and marinated tofu on the table.

"Pretty much," said Willa.

Her sister, Edith, entered the kitchen and slid into her chair. Edith was a typical Flare. "I'm not finished," she said. "Not even close, because OMG, it's Bing Day season again. I have to write a ten-page research paper."

"Zeponiah Bing was a great hero," said their mother. "I loved studying her year after year."

"I'm doing my paper on famous Flares," said Edith. "Hey, guess what! My English teacher told me about a summer program for student journalists. I'd get to go to Tornado City. Doesn't that sound awesome?"

Their father sighed. "Edith," he said, "I'm sorry, but I'm going to stop you right there."

"Why?"

"Money is tight this year."

"*Ohhhh*." Edith glared at Willa. Repairing the water damage Willa caused had been expensive. "Great. Thanks for ruining my summer, Willa. And my chance of getting into a good college. And my dreams of being a journalist."

"Edith, your dreams are not ruined," their mother said. "You can get an internship at a local paper. None of this is Willa's fault. She doesn't wet things on purpose."

"It's not my fault either, but I'm still suffering from it," Edith argued. "Isn't it time we did something to stop her from damaging everything?"

"Like what?" Willa asked. "Kick me out of the house?"

"Yes, actually! You could live in the shed! That way you'd just rain in there and not in the house!"

"Your sister is not moving into the shed," their mother said.

"Think how much better our lives would be." Edith folded her arms over her chest.

Willa swallowed.

It was cold in the shed. Plus, there was no bathroom.

And she'd be lonely.

"This conversation is over," their father pronounced. With his chin, he gestured at Edith's plate. "Eat your tofu and let's hear no more about it." He turned to Willa. "You're not going to live in the shed, okay?"

"Okay."

"And you're also not going to quarrel with your sister at the dinner table. No more of that tonight."

Willa opened her mouth to protest, but changed her mind and stayed silent. If her tears came loose, she would probably rain.

Her family might start thinking about the shed for real.

"Willa, sweetie, come watch this show with me," her mother called after dinner.

Willa followed her voice and sat down on the plastic bench that now served as their couch.

"Look at that, will you?" She gestured at the TV (which lived under a rain tarp when not in use). On-screen, a reporter stood beneath a bright red umbrella. "It's a show on special Flares in honor of Zeponiah Bing, and—oh! Your sister should watch this, too! For the essay she's writing!" She raised her voice. "Edith! Come watch!"

Willa didn't really want to watch a show about special Flares. It would just make her feel worse about her own messed-up magic.

Still, TV was better than homework.

"She is giving the traumatized citizens all the fresh water they need!" the reporter beneath the umbrella said.

The camera zoomed out to show a young woman with her arms spread and her face tilted to the sky. Her dark skin and cropped hair were dotted with raindrops. Her expression was blissful.

Willa's mother patted Willa's knee excitedly. "That's Shaylene Waterhouse, from Bimplecester, England. Look, sweetheart! She *rains*!"

The camera swept across some onlookers, who cheered. Behind them, Willa saw charred buildings, all blackened wood and sodden gray ashes.

"We love you, Shaylene!" one woman called, cupping her hands around her mouth.

The camera focused back on the reporter. "Yes, Shaylene has literally *rained* blessings on this small mining town, which still relies on well water due to its remote location. Without her magic, they never would have been able to put out the fire. She stopped the flames from spreading and saved many people's homes from destruction. Let's check in with Shaylene herself, shall we?"

The reporter approached Shaylene and asked her how she channeled her upside-down magic.

"I've always rained. My teachers didn't like me much, I'll tell you that," Shaylene said. "I was always flooding the playground, raining out kittenball games, stuff like that. But it comes naturally to me. And being upside down isn't so different from other magics. Instead of flaring, I simply rain."

Three more people were featured as the show continued. Willa watched, awestruck. All of them were able to make it rain outdoors, and all were labeled by the reporter as Upside-Down Flares. Shaylene Waterhouse was a firefighter. Two others helped during droughts, when people couldn't grow crops. And one had created an oasis in the desert and built a fancy resort hotel in a green meadow where previously there'd been nothing but dust.

"Worldwide, there are only four known raining Upside-Down Flares," the reporter stated. "Just Waterhouse, Keats, Birdy, and Carpenter-Balliwash."

Willa registered the reporter's claim—only four, and no more.

The reporter was wrong, though! Because *Willa* had this magic, or something like it.

More important, those grown-up Upside-Down Flares were powerful! And awesome. They used their rain, and people loved them for it!

"They're like you, Willa!" her mother exclaimed.

"Are they, though?" Edith said sourly. "They rain *outside*. Where people actually *want* rain. Seems totally different to me."

"Edith!" their mother scolded.

"I'd rather be a typical Flare any day," Edith said. "That's all I'm saying."

Well, Willa would rather be a typical Flare, too.

But maybe . . . maybe one day she would rain outside like Shaylene Waterhouse.

8

The next day, Ms. Starr took the UDM kids to the school library to research their Bing Day projects. Nory brought a pencil case with supplies. Scissors. Markers. Glitter.

She wanted her poster to be Outstanding. No, she wanted it to be Marvelous.

What if one day the teachers gave out Ms? What if they gave Nory the first-ever M?!

The librarian, Mr. Wang, was a koala, at least for the moment. He was perched on top of a very high shelf, organizing books.

"Hello, Goodwin!" called Ms. Starr. "I brought my class. We're all excited about Bing Day research."

"Are we?" Sebastian muttered.

"It depends on how you define *excited*," Pepper muttered back. "If *excited* means *miserably bored*, then sure."

Koala–Mr. Wang clambered down the shelf and fluxed into human form. He was tall and reed thin, with balding black hair and a fondness for turtleneck sweaters.

"Hi, Eloise," he said. "Hi, kids. What a treat this project is! There are so many directions your research can take you. What are your topics?"

"Old-timey snacks," Elliott volunteered. "Bax and I want to know what people ate and how it was cooked."

"Fantastic," Mr. Wang said. "Perhaps cookbooks from the 1890s would get you started? You can find several historical cookbooks in the food and cookery section." He pointed. "Next?"

He directed Pepper and Andres toward the education section, where they could look up single-sex schools. Sebastian and Marigold went to the archives to look for articles on the history of parades.

When everyone else was sorted, Mr. Wang looked expectantly at Nory and Willa.

"We're going to explore weather conditions leading to big freeze of 1893," Nory said, trying to sound enthusiastic. She wasn't actually interested in storm patterns. She just wanted to do the best possible job on the project. Storm patterns had been the only topic Willa had seemed remotely interested in.

Mr. Wang clasped his hands together. "Terrific! Terrific! Begin in the Earth Science section, there, at the back of the library."

"Thanks," Nory said. "Come on, Willa. Let's go."

In the Earth Science section, Nory pulled potential books off the shelves. *Weather Patterns. Understanding Weather.*

Willa stood there, blinking. Doing nothing.

"Oysters on toast!" Nory heard Elliott cry from the cookery section. "Gross!"

Nory wished he were her partner, but she tried to look on the bright side. There were lots of books here! This almanac would be perfect! She opened it and flipped through the pages.

"Are you going to help?" she asked Willa. "We should look up average temperatures for this time of year. And . . . I don't know what else, actually. Information about blizzards?"

Grudgingly, Willa pulled a book from the shelves.

They read in silence. Graphs and numbers swam in front of Nory's eyes.

Sheesh, weather was boring. She could hear Marigold and Sebastian chattering as they ran back and forth from the shelves to the photocopier.

"Flare jugglers are fascinating," said Sebastian.

"I know, right?" replied Marigold.

Willa looked up from her book. "I don't really know what we're concentrating on," she said. "What should I be doing right now?"

"Isn't it obvious?" Nory snapped. "Take notes! Get an idea for our poster! Find out something interesting about weather!"

"It's not that interesting."

"Excuse me? *You* chose it!"

"I didn't choose anything!"

"Just do your share of the work and let's not talk about it," Nory said.

"Fine," said Willa. She sat down and opened her book again.

Elliott was photocopying pictures of asparagus on toast.

Marigold was watching videos of Flare jugglers and marching bands.

Nory went to get her poster board from Ms. Starr. She brought over her scissors, markers, and glitter. "I'm going to use some sparkles to make a blizzard," she told Willa. "That can be a background for a chart about temperatures."

She copied out some numbers from the almanac and carefully applied glitter, while Willa read quietly.

"How's it going?" Nory asked eventually. "Do you have an idea for what else to put on the poster?"

"Not really," Willa said.

"Not really? How is that helpful?"

Willa shook her head.

A drop of water landed smack in the middle of the poster board.

No, no, no.

"Don't cry! You'll soak our project!" Nory moved the poster out of the way.

"I'm not crying," said Willa.

Another drop landed right in the glitter. Then another.

Three more drops landed on one of the weather books.

"You are so!" said Nory. "Look!"

"I know you think I'm a crybaby," snapped Willa. "But sometimes my rain has nothing to do with tears. Other Upside-Down Flares don't cry when they rain. I saw them on TV. And look at my face. I am NOT

CRYING." Willa took a breath. "And besides, this isn't even rain. It's just a drizzle."

A few more drops came down.

"I don't think you're a crybaby," Nory said.

"I *know* you do."

The way Willa said *know* made Nory flush.

Willa knew! She knew what Nory had said! Elliott must have told her!

Nory turned her back on Willa and stomped over to where Elliott sat with Bax.

"Did you tell Willa I called her a crybaby?" she demanded.

Elliott winced. "I didn't mean to! It just came out."

"Elliott! That was a private conversation!"

Elliott looked behind Nory to Willa. "Willa! I can't believe you told Nory what I said!"

"I didn't mean to!" Willa said.

Nory narrowed her eyes. "It happened while she was *crying*."

"Drizzling!" Willa yelled.

"What's going on, kids?" Ms. Starr asked, coming over. "Everyone okay?"

Willa looked like she was about to burst. "I need to go outside so I don't rain!"

"Of course, Willa. Go ahead."

Willa ran out the library door that led into the schoolyard. The drizzling inside the library stopped as soon as she was outdoors.

Nory turned to Elliott. "I can't believe you told her. Not cool."

"You shouldn't put me in the middle," he said. "And I told you not to label people!"

Ms. Starr put a hand on Nory's shoulder. "I know you two are very good friends. Would you like to do some deep-breathing exercises together?"

"No, thank you," said Elliott.

"Really, no, thank you," said Nory. At that, they both laughed, just a little.

"Then please figure out a way to get along," said Ms. Starr.

"We do get along!" Nory protested. "Elliott and I get along fine. It's Willa who—" She broke off.

Elliott glanced away.

"Well, I trust you to be mature about the situation," Ms. Starr said. "*All* of you."

Hmph.

Nory didn't want to be mature. She wanted to yell some more! Or turn into a dritten and breathe fire!

Bax came to the rescue. "Nory, look!" he said. "People used to make homemade liver sausage." He pointed to a recipe in a book.

Nory was glad for a distraction. She leaned over to see. "That is super disgusting."

"Do you want to see oysters on toast?" asked Bax. "There's a picture of that one."

"They put everything on toast back then," said Elliott. "They were obsessed with toast."

The oysters on toast looked like slimy eyeballs. "Eeewwwwww," said Nory.

She peeked at Elliott. She could tell he felt bad about telling Willa what she'd said.

And she *did* feel bad about calling Willa a crybaby.

"Look," she said, pointing. "Mushroom ketchup!"

"Mushroom ketchup!" cried Elliott. "Bax, Nory found the perfect gross food to round out our poster!"

Nory sat down with the two boys for the rest of the period. They talked about mushroom ketchup and celery soda and barley water.

By the time the bell rang, she and Elliott were friends again.

Willa sat on a bench and watched some sixth-grade Flyers play a game of fly-ball. She knew her class had gone to lunch, but she didn't feel like eating with the UDM kids. She didn't feel like eating, period.

Well, maybe just her cookie.

After a few minutes, Marigold appeared and sat down next to her. "You okay?"

Willa shrugged. "My magic is annoying. Most of the time, I wish I didn't even have it."

Marigold nodded. "I used to feel like that, too." She tucked her hair behind her ears. Willa caught a glimpse of her small, skin-toned hearing aid.

Willa considered this news. Marigold shrank things. There was no label for her magic. None of the five Fs was the opposite of shrinking. How would it feel to be Marigold and have a type of magic that wasn't even upside down?!

"The night before the parent-teacher conferences," Marigold said, "I had a dream that Ms. Starr told me that I had fitting magic. Like, I was a Fitter."

"*Fitting* magic? I've never heard of it."

"Neither had I. But I thought, oh, fitting magic has to do with size! That's me! I have that! And I woke up feeling amazing. I mean, I know it's not a thing. But it got me thinking. What if there are more than five types of magic?"

Willa arched her brows. "There aren't." She ticked them off on her fingers. "Flare, Flyer, Fluxer, Flicker, Fuzzy."

"Maybe. But what if you have water magic?" Marigold pressed. "You and Elliott. I'm not saying you do! Just . . ."

"What if," Willa whispered.

It would make sense. She didn't have weak Flare magic, like Elliott did. She had no flare at all. She'd believed everyone when they labeled her an Upside-Down Flare, because the people who said that were her parents and her teachers.

But what if?

"Maybe I'm an . . . Aqua talent?" she tried. "I can do things with waves in tutoring. Just tiny things, but I can do them."

Marigold nodded. "It's good to give it a name, I think. But we need it to start with F. A Flater." She said "Flater" to rhyme with "water." She shook her head. "No, that sounds too much like Farter."

Willa snorted.

"A Fountain," Marigold said. "A Fizz? A Fishie?"

Willa snorted again. And laughed. "Please not Fishie."

"Okay," said Marigold. "Well, keep thinking."

"I like that you might be a Fitter. But you know what else you are? It also starts with an F."

"Fashionable?" Marigold joked. "Fiddling? Wait, I don't fiddle."

"Fun!" said Willa. "You're definitely f-u-n *fun*. I'm really glad you're my friend."

"*Friend* starts with an *F*, too," Marigold said, and she rested her head on Willa's shoulder.

9

Aunt Margo was using her Flyer magic to unload the dishwasher. She flew the dishes into the cupboards. Meanwhile, she was doing a crossword puzzle.

Nory sat at the kitchen table, flipping through the weather books she'd brought home from the library. She lifted a corner of the water-damaged poster board and let it fall. How was she supposed to fix this? She hated this project. Hated it!

"AAAHHHHH!" yelled Nory. "I'm never going to get an O with the paper all warped like this!"

Three plates fell to the floor with a clatter.

Aunt Margo gave Nory a look.

"Sorry," squeaked Nory.

"Well, that's why we have plastic plates," Aunt Margo said. "But why the yelling?"

Nory scowled. "I hate my Bing Day project."

Aunt Margo put down her pencil and stood up. "Let's go for a fly. Sometimes fresh air changes your mood. And the height helps change your perspective." She wrapped a thick wool scarf around her neck. "Get your coat. It's cold out."

Nory did as she was told. On the edge of the front porch, Aunt Margo held out her hand. "Ready?"

"Ready."

Aunt Margo bent her knees and launched both herself and Nory into the velvety sky. Up they went, above the houses, above the trees.

The stars were glorious. They twinkled and winked. Below, the town lights sparkled. Nory's ribs loosened.

"Perspective!" Aunt Margo said over the rush of the wind. She squeezed Nory's hand. "The whole world is spread out beneath us, and every person in every house has stuff to deal with. Everyone! But flying helps, don't you think?"

Nory returned Aunt Margo's squeeze. It *did* help. It did and did and did.

They flew over Bing Society Memorial Museum. "We're going there on Wednesday," Nory said.

"I know! And next week's the parade," said Aunt Margo. "Are you excited?"

"Honestly?" Nory said. "I love parades, but I pretty much hate Zeponiah Bing right now."

"Why?"

"All she does is cause me problems!"

Aunt Margo glanced at Nory. "What about Gertrude Raspberry?" she asked. "Surely you don't hate Gertrude Raspberry."

"I might hate her. Who *is* Gertrude Raspberry?"

"Raspberry was Bing's amazing Fluxer friend. You don't know about her? I think you'll love her." Aunt Margo tilted to the right, and they flew over the park. The trees were dense and dark.

"If you say so," Nory said doubtfully. "No one's mentioned her."

"In that case, I'll fill you in," said Aunt Margo. "Gertrude Raspberry was Zeponiah Bing's partner. They met when Zeponiah was in college and lived together afterward."

"Partner?"

Aunt Margo nodded. "Her life companion, yes. Gertrude was a Fluxer, quite a good one. She did large carnivores. Anyway, she's the one who read about Dunwiddle's Great Frost in the newspaper. It was Gertrude who convinced Zeponiah that only she could help. Zeponiah didn't want to come back to her hometown after so many years away—but Gertrude convinced Zeponiah that we needed her. So they used most of their savings to buy train tickets. And do you know what happened?"

"What?"

"The train got stuck. Because of all the snow! And then Gertrude fluxed into a polar bear and carried Zeponiah all the way to Dunwiddle, where Bing used her amazing Flare powers to save the crops and warm the whole town."

"Why couldn't the Dunwiddle Flares save the town?"

"Their magic wasn't strong enough. Bing saved so many lives. But none of it would have happened without Gertrude!"

Nory pictured a giant polar bear trudging through peaks of snow, her life companion clinging bravely to her fur. "Okay, I *do* like Gertrude," she said.

"Told you so," Aunt Margo said. She shivered, and announced it was time to head home.

As they flew back to the house, Nory couldn't stop thinking about Polar-Bear-Gertrude. She felt hopeful for the first time in days.

No more boring storm patterns!

No more graphs or charts!

She and Willa would do their report on Gertrude. A wonderful Fluxer and a brave and true friend.

Aunt Margo landed in the front yard. Nory bounced on her toes. She felt tingly and excited. Flying really had changed her mood. "Aunt Margo, could we take Elliott flying?"

"Sure. Why?"

"Elliott's never flown with you, and I think he'd really like it."

"We can find a time this weekend."

"He's visiting his grandparents this weekend. Could we do Monday? What time do you start work? Could you fly Elliott and me to school? But, like, the long way around so that it's fun?" The words spilled out.

After what had happened in the library today, Nory really wanted to do something nice for Elliott. After all, he had been right when he said she shouldn't call Willa names. And he had been right that she shouldn't put him in the middle. Now he needed to remember what a good friend Nory could be.

"I'd be glad to fly you and Elliott to school on Monday," said Aunt Margo.

"Great!" Nory grinned. "It'll be a surprise!"

Nory was pretty sure Elliott wasn't mad anymore. But it wouldn't hurt to do something nice for him. Just the two of them, together.

10

Willa got to school early on Monday morning. She'd spent the weekend thinking about Marigold's idea about water magic. Now she wanted to talk to Ms. Starr about it.

But Ms. Starr wasn't in her classroom. Only Carrot was. The bunny sat on her hind legs in the center of Ms. Starr's desk, nibbling a piece of lettuce. "If you're looking for Eloise, she's in a meeting."

Willa said good morning and unpacked her backpack, stacking her notebooks in her desk.

"Is there something you were hoping to discuss?" the bunny persisted.

"Not really," Willa said.

"You can talk to me, you know," urged Carrot.

Willa shook her head. "It's about magic."

"I help Pepper with her magic. In fact, I go to all of Pepper's tutoring sessions. Did you know that?"

"I know you're, like, the only animal who isn't afraid of Pepper's Fierce magic," Willa said. "You must be awfully brave."

"Not exactly," said Carrot. She swallowed her last bite of lettuce and groomed her whiskers. "It's more that I've learned how to navigate my fear."

Willa didn't understand.

"Most animals feel a jolt of fear and run," Carrot elaborated. "Me? I get a jolt of fear, and I'm like, *Oh, yeah, there's a jolt of fear. Hello, fear!* It's still there, but I don't let it bother me."

"Wow."

"It took practice," said Carrot. "When I was little, my mother adopted a fox cub. She raised us as sisters, and I'm sure that helped." She eyed Willa. "Rabbits and foxes don't usually mix, but she was my sister. She still is! You can't be afraid of your own sister, am I right?"

Willa furrowed her brow. She was scared of Edith sometimes.

"Anyway, if you don't mind my saying, you could practice the same thing," Carrot continued.

"What?"

"Your emotions! You could practice feeling them, but not letting them bother you so much. If you feel sad, for example, you could say, 'Hello, sadness. I see you there.' And then, hopefully—"

"I wouldn't rain," Willa concluded.

"I think you rain when you're upset," said Carrot.

"I do."

"And, as it stands, you can't help getting upset."

"No, I can't."

"But perhaps you could learn to navigate it. You could navigate your sadness just as I navigate my fear."

"Can you teach me how?" Willa asked.

"Of course! It's a matter of stepping back and taking note of your emotions. 'I'm afraid right now.' 'I'm angry right now.' 'I want to cry right now.' That's step one. Then, over time, you'll master step two. That's deciding what you want to do with those emotions. You'll always feel them. That doesn't go away. But if you can feel what you're feeling and still hold on to a level of calm, it's a useful power to have."

Willa heard what Carrot was saying, but she wasn't sure the concept applied to her. Carrot was an adult bunny, after all. Maybe the whole "staying calm while feeling your feelings" thing was more for grown-ups than kids.

"How did Pepper learn to pause her fiercing?" she asked. Because Pepper could do that now. Pepper could be around animals and not scare them, pausing her magic for as much as a couple of minutes.

"That's one thing we work on in tutoring," Carrot answered. "I told her to think of her magic as a river.

That's step one. Step two? Imagine a dam, closing across the water and holding back the flow, pinching shut. You might only be able to hold back the river for a short time, but a short time is better than not at all."

Wow.

Willa could already start and stop her tiny rain clouds. But rain that stemmed from her emotions was big rain, and not on purpose. When it happened, Willa couldn't control it.

But if Pepper could pause her magic . . . maybe Willa could pause hers, too?

"Like damming a river?" she repeated.

"It's a metaphor," said Carrot. "But you get the idea. Hey, do you have any radishes?"

"No, but I have an apple," said Willa. She pulled it out of her backpack and showed it to Carrot.

"Put it on the desk."

Willa hesitated. The apple was for her lunch. But she did what Carrot said. Maybe the bunny was going to show her another important magic technique.

Instead, Carrot pressed on the apple with her two front paws and took a bite. Then another and another.

"Hey!" Willa cried. She hadn't meant for Carrot to eat the apple! Now she'd be hungry later.

Hold on, she told herself. *Take note of your emotions.* That's what Carrot had said.

She thought, *I'm angry right now. I'm so angry I feel like crying!*

Then she thought, *Hello, Weepy Anger. I see you there.*

She thought, *That bunny tricked you out of your apple and you're stinkin' mad. Hello, Stinkin' Mad. I see you there!*

She still felt angry.

Well, annoyed.

But she didn't feel tears at the edge of her eyes. The frustration at losing her apple was no longer so loud inside her head.

"Good apple," Carrot commented. "Crunchy."

Carrot was really, really cute. It was hard to stay mad at such a cute rabbit.

And, okay, now Willa knew that Carrot would take a kid's fruit. Lesson learned.

"You talked me out of my apple, you tricky rabbit," she said.

"I haven't had an apple in days," said Carrot. "Mm-mm-mm."

"Next time you could just *ask*," said Willa. "I nearly rained on you just now."

"But you didn't," said Carrot. "Not one drop."

Elliott was the second person to walk into Ms. Starr's classroom. His curly hair had a dent in it from the hat he'd worn to school.

He swung by Carrot and held up his hand for a high five. Carrot looked surprised but lifted her paw. Next he stopped by Willa's desk.

She slapped his upraised palm, even though he'd yelled at her on Friday.

"I'm glad I got you alone," said Elliott.

"She's not alone," said Carrot. "Bunnies are people, too, you know."

"Sorry, Carrot. I meant, I wanted to talk to Willa without the other kids around." He gulped. "I'm sorry I yelled at you, Willa."

"It's okay," said Willa. "I'm sorry I told Nory you told me what she said. I guess I did put you in a bad spot."

"I didn't walk to school with Nory today. I didn't want to talk to her until after I talked to you." Elliott frowned. "But I just want to make clear: I'm friends with *everybody*. No taking sides between you and Nory. And I hope you won't say mean stuff about each other. At least not when I can hear."

"That seems fair," Willa said. "So long as Nory keeps to her end of the bargain."

11

While Elliott and Willa talked, Nory waited for Elliott to show up to walk to school with her.

She waited. And waited. And waited.

So did Aunt Margo. They were going to surprise Elliott with a flight over the town!

But Elliott never showed up.

Later, when Nory arrived at school on her own, she was worried. Was Elliott home sick? Had something happened to him on his way to her house?

She worried while she put her stuff in her locker. She worried while she got a drink of water at the invisible water fountain. She worried while she dodged Flyers and stepped over a group of Fluxers who were practicing hamsters in the hallways. But when she entered the UDM classroom and saw that Elliott was already there, her worry turned into something else.

She set down her poster board and marched over to him. "Elliott Cohen! I waited and waited for you!"

Elliott looked startled. "I . . . uh . . . came to school early," he said.

"How was I supposed to know that?"

"I don't know," Elliott said feebly. He glanced over at Willa, who was stroking Carrot's ears. "It's not like we signed a contract saying we'd walk to school together every single day."

Sebastian looked over at them. "People," he said. "Your voices are making very sharp sound waves and they are hurting my eyes."

Nory ignored him. "But, Elliott! Aunt Margo was going to fly us to school! She was going to tour us *all around town* before we got here. I arranged it *specially* for this morning as a surprise!"

Elliott glanced at Willa. *Again.* "I'm sorry."

Nory seethed.

Why did he keep glancing at Willa?

Was he walking to school with *her* now?

"Good morning, class!" Ms. Starr called, striding into the classroom and closing the door. "Who's ready for some semaphore work?"

Everyone groaned. Semaphore work meant communicating—or trying to communicate—with someone by waving flags.

"Pair up, kids, and grab a flag," Ms. Starr went on. "As always, try to connect with your partner without words. I'm taping the list of signals we've practiced here on the bulletin board. Nonverbal communication is a skill that will help you with your magic."

"Elliott?" Willa said. "Partners?"

"Sure," he answered.

Nory's mouth fell open. Willa *knew* Nory was upset about Elliott missing the flying outing. She *knew*! And she still asked him to be her partner! And he still said yes! Where was the consideration?

"Nory, partners?" Pepper asked.

Nory turned. "Of course," she told Pepper loudly. "I would love to be your semaphore partner, Pepper. You are a good friend. I always have fun with you."

Pepper looked at her funny. "Why are you using a robot voice?"

"What? I'm not!" Nory grabbed a flag and pulled Pepper to the middle of the floor. "Let's communicate nonverbally. Come on." Then she gave Willa the stink eye.

At lunch, Elliott ate with Willa.

Okay, Elliott ate with Willa *and* Bax *and* Marigold *and* Sebastian.

But not with Nory. Nory was on duty for keeping Andres safe on his leash, so she ate with him and Pepper.

At recess, Elliott played soccer with Willa, Bax, and some kids from the Fuzzy class, while Nory, Pepper, and Andres hung out at the swing set.

Grrr.

Still, Nory tried to look on the bright side. She and Pepper each had a swing, and two swings plus Andres meant they could play a game they had invented after their trip to Dragon Haven a couple of weeks ago. Swinging meant Pepper and Nory could pretend to fly, too. In the game, Andres was a Flyer named Lars Ernesto Montmorency. The two girls were flying dragons who helped him rescue animals in peril.

Nory was a Blurper Dragon, of course. Her name was Rocket. Pepper was a Luminous Dragonette named Pingleton.

Anyway, it was a pretty fun recess after all, but when they went indoors, Ms. Starr told everyone to work on their Bing projects.

Nory's insides coiled. She hadn't yet told Willa about the change in topic.

"I solved our boringness problem!" she told Willa brightly as she got out the poster board and put it between them on the table. "We're changing subjects and it's going to be so much better. Listen. Are you ready?" Willa didn't say anything, so Nory pressed on. "We're doing Gertrude Raspberry, the amazing Fluxer!"

Willa made a sour face. "I found some more books on storms," she complained. "I was going to read them."

"Did you read them *yet*?" Nory actually hoped Willa hadn't.

"Not much of them," Willa admitted.

"Great. Gertrude is way more exciting than weather and she'll make a much better poster. There's a ton of information about her, so we can have extra sources and get an O. Don't you want to get an O?"

Willa looked confused. "But we started the poster board already. With the glitter. I don't think we're allowed to take a new one."

"Omigosh, it'll be fine," Nory snapped. "What's your problem? You hadn't read anything for the weather project, anyway."

Willa flushed. She blinked her eyes.

Nory knew that blink. It meant she had better be gentle, because if Willa started raining, everyone's posters would be ruined. She placed her palms on the table and made a big effort to soften her tone. "Do you know about Gertrude? She's really awesome."

"I know a little," Willa said.

"Yay! That means it won't be hard. We can write facts about her life and make a map of Gertrude and Zeponiah's journey from Florida to Dunwiddle. We'll paint a polar bear here, where the glitter is. So the glitter can still be a snowstorm, and we can use the same piece of poster board. See?"

Willa nodded.

Nory refrained from mentioning the water-damaged corner. *Bygones*, she told herself grimly. "All right, then let's get started," she said. "Our poster has to be finished by Friday."

"I know the due date," Willa said.

Nory mentally reviewed the week ahead. "I got books about her from the Dunwiddle library this weekend. We have at least five sources. We'll have most of tomorrow to work on it. Wednesday we have our field trip to the Bing museum, so we might not get time then. But we can finish up on Thursday and Friday."

"Elliott and I have AquaMerge tutoring on Tuesday and Thursday," said Willa.

Who cared about AquaMerge?

Tutoring had nothing to do with this project!

Why did Willa always bring up tutoring with Elliott? Big deal. She got to hang out with Elliott in the pool.

What a show-off.

"I have a really good idea," Nory told Coach Vitomin at the end of the day.

"Tell me!" Coach said. He tossed a piece of raw broccoli into the air and caught it in his mouth.

"Tomorrow we should work on my squippy."

"What's your squippy?"

"A squid-puppy. I've done it before by accident, but I don't have it under control yet."

"Nory, you can't play kittenball as a squid-puppy."

"I think practicing other animals would be good for me."

"Other *kitten* variations, sure. Keep your head in the game."

Nory thought fast. "What about a squitten? A squid-kitten could be good for kittenball."

Coach looked unconvinced. "How do you figure that?"

"Coach. C'mon. I could use my tentacles. I could suction my opponents with all my extra limbs."

Coach wrinkled his brow.

"Think big, Coach," Nory said. "Eight legs instead of four. Imagine what I could accomplish."

"Are you sure you can do a squitten?" Coach asked.

No, Nory was not.

"Absolutely!" she said.

He scratched his bald head. "Then what the heck. Sure, tomorrow we'll work on your squitten."

Nory clapped. "Let's meet at *the pool*!"

"The pool? *What* pool?"

"The high school pool! Some of the other UDM kids are in there at the same time we meet for tutoring, so I'm sure we can swim then, too. I'll tell Bax. We'll bring bathing suits!" Bax and Nory both had Coach for a tutor.

"Or you could practice squippy in a bucket," Coach said. "If Bax fluxes into a rock while we're at the pool, he'll sink."

"No, no, a bucket's no good," Nory said quickly. "You can help Bax work on something that floats! Like a boat! Or a rubber duckie! And you can show us how to do a fish. You can do a fish, right, Coach?"

Coach puffed up his chest. "Can I do a fish?! Of course I can do a fish! Fish are complicated, but I can do them." He made a fist and drove it into his opposite palm.

Nory gave him a thumbs-up and hurried out the door before he changed his mind.

12

Tuesday afternoon, Willa skipped out of the changing room and toward the pool.

After her talk with Marigold a few days ago, she'd done a lot of thinking. Now she had a ton of questions for Ms. C. She wanted to talk about Marigold's "other types of magic" theory. She was also hoping to try Carrot's technique of damming shut the river of her magic.

Willa had even read one of the books on Gertrude. She'd taken notes, too. She'd been too nervous to show her notes to Nory in case Nory criticized her handwriting or said they weren't detailed enough, but she'd taken them. She planned to surprise Nory with a cool fact: Gertrude flunked her polar bear license test the first time around.

Now, at the pool, Willa hung her towel on the hook and tugged at her bathing suit bottom. Today she was wearing her pink bikini, which was another reason it was a good day. She loved her pink bikini.

"Come on in!" Elliott called from the water.

"Yes, go ahead and swim for a bit," called Ms. C from the bleachers. She glanced up from a portfolio she was looking over. "I'll be right with you two."

"Awesome." Willa dove into the pool and swam to the shallow end.

Hi, water, she said silently, coming up for air. She swooshed her hands over its surface. Each finger left a ripple in its wake.

She twirled, her arms outstretched. Swirls of water circled her. The beauty of it reminded her of the peaceful feeling she got when she read poetry. Being in the water gave her the same poem-y feeling.

Ms. C came over five minutes later. "Okay, kids," she said, settling on the edge with her feet and shins in the pool. "Shall we start with Bubbles?"

Willa swam over. "Actually, I was hoping we could talk," she said. "I have some questions."

"Sure."

"Do you know Marigold Ramos? She's in Ms. Starr's UDM class with Elliott and me. We were talking, and Marigold dreamed she was a—"

The door to the pool swung open.

"Surprise!" Nory cried. She stood in the doorway. Behind her stood Bax and Coach. All three wore swimsuits.

What?!

Why was *Nory* here?!

"I can't believe you dragged us to the pool," Bax muttered to Nory. "I told you I can't swim."

"You told me you swim a little," Nory said. "And this is a good chance for you to learn!"

"I really don't want to turn into a rock in the water," said Bax.

"I have a floatie for you," said Coach. "And Ms. Cruciferous and I both have lifeguard certifications."

Bax tightened his jaw.

"Watch this!" Nory called. She ran forward and cannonballed into the pool.

Willa seethed.

This is the best, Nory thought. Why hadn't she come up with this idea before? All her tutoring sessions from now on should take place in the pool!

She, Coach, and Bax were in the shallow end. Elliott, Willa, and Ms. C had moved to the deep end, but even so, Nory could wave at Elliott throughout the lesson! He was waving back at her right now! Clearly, he was glad his very best friend was in the pool with him.

"This is not comfortable," Bax complained from his floatie, which was shaped like a rainbow unicorn. His bottom was wedged into the hole of it. He flapped his arms helplessly.

"Bax, my boy, you're doing great!" Coach exclaimed.

"What makes you say that?"

"Why, you're staying human in a difficult situation, of course!"

"Can I please just sit on the edge of the pool?"

"Listen, Bax," said Coach. "Right now you're in a place where you might flux, but take stock of yourself! You're breathing deeply. You're maintaining focus. You're using the techniques Ms. Starr and I have taught you to keep yourself human!"

"If I flux into a piano right now, we'll be in serious trouble," Bax muttered.

"Ah, but that's why we're in the shallow end," said Coach. "You're always an *upright* piano! Part of you will be above water!"

Bax looked at Coach as if he were nuts. "And that's supposed to make me feel better *why*?"

"Nory, I'm going to show you some basics of squid fluxing," Coach told her. "Are you ready? Paying attention?"

Nory was.

Coach wrinkled his brow and made a bearing-down expression.

Nothing happened.

"Whenever you're ready!" Nory said. She was psyched to see Coach do squid. She had never seen any fish fluxing at all, actually.

A flush crept up Coach's thick neck. Soon his entire face was red. Then his bald head turned red.

"Coach?" Nory asked. "Are you okay?"

"I'm mainly a mammal Fluxer," Coach said. "I specialize in felines, really."

"But yesterday, when we talked—"

"Give me a second, will you?" Coach said. He grunted. Then—*pop!* His right arm turned into a squid arm. Or a squid leg? Whichever.

A vein pulsed in Coach's neck, and his other arm fluxed into a second squid leg.

Squid-Coach frowned. His squid arms—*legs*—seemed to have a life of their own. They flopped and swelled. His right squid leg-arm slapped the water, and Bax drew back.

"Aaaargh!" Squid-Coach growled, straining with all his might. With a ripping sound, two more squid legs emerged where his human legs used to be.

"Maybe if you had all eight tentacles, you'd be more balanced?" Nory suggested. She felt a little sorry for him and wanted his squid to come out well.

Squid-Coach swam in a circle, his squid limbs flailing. He resembled a sundial, Nory thought. A wet, floppy, bald-headed sundial. Nory edged closer to Bax. "Yikes," Bax muttered.

Squid-Coach waved all four tentacles furiously, churning the water into a froth. "I heard that!"

"Sorry, Coach," Bax called. "Just, you're kind of a torso with tentacles."

With a *whoosh*, Squid-Coach took in a gulp of air, flung up his tentacles, and sank beneath the water. When he rose, he was back to his regular teacher shape.

"Hmm," Coach said. "That didn't go as planned." He turned toward Bax. "How are *you* doing, Bax? Still human?"

"Still human," Bax said from the unicorn floatie.

"Fantastic." Coach clasped his hands. "Nory, you're up. Don't worry if you can't get all eight legs on your first go. In fact, for kittenball, it might prove helpful to keep your front kitten legs, but add on squid tentacles." Coach scratched his head. "But will you be able to swim?" He shrugged. "We don't know. But I'm standing by. I won't let you drown. Are you ready?"

"Hey, Elliott!" Nory called. "I'm going to try squitten!"

Elliott didn't turn around. He was listening to his tutor.

Nory tried again. "Elliott! Watch!"

He glanced her way.

Okay, then. Ready. Set. Go! Nory raised her hands over her head and stretched her spine. Energy crackled through her. The world went fuzzy as her body—at least, half of it—went furry.

Squitten-Nory was here! She had a kitten head. She could tell by the whiskers. She had a kitten torso, too. But sticking out from her torso were four legs-turned-tentacles and one tail-turned-tentacle!

Five tentacles! *Five!*

"You did it, Nory!" Coach cried.

Squitten-Nory felt fantastic. She paddled with her head above water for a minute. Was Elliott looking? Could he see from all the way in the deep end?

She popped back to girl form and looked over.

Elliott was talking to Willa.

"Elliott, did you see? I did squitten!"

Ms. C held her finger to her lips.

Was she *shushing* Nory? She was! She was! And Elliott had missed the squitten!

Ms. C turned her attention back to her students. All three held on to the pool's edge, their expressions serious.

"All right," Coach said. "Squitten accomplished! I know you have gym class starting soon, so let's dry off."

No way! Nory thought. *Elliott didn't even see!*

Before Coach could make eye contact with her, Nory fisted her hands and concentrated with all her might. *Squitten, squitten, squitten!*

Bones cracked. Muscles stretched. *Squelch!*

Ha-ha-ha, look at me! Squitten-Nory thought, swimming hard. She paddled to the rope that separated the shallow end of the pool from the deep end. She slapped a tentacle on the water's surface.

Elliott didn't look over.

Meow!

He still didn't look over. He kept talking to Willa!

Hiss!

Then Squitten-Nory felt a new and unpleasant sensation. *Pip, pip, pip!* Prickly quills were exploding out of the rear part of her body.

What?

Pip, pip, pip! Quills came out of her forehead and her front paws, too.

Oh, dear. She was adding porcupine to her squitten!

What the zum-zum?

Stop! Do not add porcupine! No one wants a squitten with quills!

Calm down.

Control your magic. Think of the semaphore! Think of the poetry!

Pip, pip, PIP! Semaphore and poetry were no help. More quills came out.

Nory could feel her squid tentacles sucking back into her body.

Zwingo! Now she had no legs at all, kitten, squid, or otherwise.

Swoosh, brr-r-r-oonk, swooop!

Her body lengthened out. Fins stretched from her back and sides. A powerful tail swished behind her. She could tell she had gotten huge. And those angry, jealous, sticky, prickly porcupine pins kept stabbing their way out of her! They jabbed out of her whole entire body!

"For the love of green tea, what *is* she?" Coach cried.

Nory knew the answer. She could feel it.

She was a dolphin with porcupine quills. She was Porcuphin-Nory.

Porcuphin!

Wheee! Porcuphin-Nory zoomed through the water like a balloon that had just been untied.

Whoosh!

She saw a large fleshy thing, so she poked it. Someone bellowed.

Porcuphin-Nory zipped away! She found something squishy and brightly colored. She poked *it*, and zzzzzzz!

She heard the sound of air escaping, and another bellow!

Then a *thunk*. Something large and rocklike hit the bottom of the pool.

All sorts of bellows echoed around her. Male bellows, female bellows, kid bellows. Too much!

She zigged away from the arms trying to contain her. In the depths of the water, she saw something pink. The word *bikini* floated into her porcuphin mind, then just as quickly dissolved. *Bikini?* What was *bikini?*

She needed to poke the *bikini* thing! She rocketed forward and poke-poke-poked. The *bikini* thing thrashed. Splashes! Screams! Chaos!

"Get me out of here!" a girl's voice called.

"Stop that . . . giant puffer fish!" a man's voice called.

Giant puffer fish? *Puffer* fish?!

Porcuphin-Nory was offended.

"The rock!" a man cried. "SAVE THE ROCK! He can't swim!"

"Everyone out!" called a woman. "I'm draining the pool!"

Everything swam before Porcuphin-Nory's eyes. Water gurgled and swirled, gurgled and swirled, until . . . where did it all go?

Porcuphin-Nory flailed on the damp cement. The air, chilly on her flesh, brought Nory back to her human senses, and *sloop*!

Nory fluxed back into her normal self.

She looked up at Coach, Willa, and Ms. C. They seemed very far away. Coach was red-faced and breathing hard, leaning forward with his palms on his thighs. Willa was wearing a pink bikini, and she was clutching her backside as if it hurt.

"That was a disaster," Coach scolded. "A complete and utter disaster."

"You drained the pool," Nory stated.

"*I* drained the pool," said Ms. C.

"Nory!" barked Coach. "You derailed our lesson, you lost control of your human mind, and you popped Bax's floatie!"

"Bax?" Nory looked around. "Is he okay? Where is he?"

"He fluxed. Elliott took him to the nurse in the wheelbarrow." Coach stared at her. "He'll be all right, but only because I was brave enough to dive into the pool despite the presence of a . . . a . . ."

"Porcuphin," Nory supplied. She climbed out of the pool.

"I made a mistake coming here," Coach told Ms. C. "We disrupted your class and put you at risk. I'm sorry."

Nory shivered. Coach had never sounded disappointed in her before.

"Nory, apologize to Willa and Ms. C," he said.

"Sorry," she said in a small voice.

They nodded, but didn't speak. Ms. C gestured to Willa, and they left.

"I don't know what's going on with you, Nory," said Coach when they were gone, "but that wasn't a lesson. That was . . . I don't know. Showing off, acting crazy—something like that."

"I was trying to be marvelous!" she protested.

"Well, stop," he said. "I'm all for expanding your potential, but that was unacceptable and rude." He pulled a porcuphin quill out of his foot and limped toward the men's changing room, leaving Nory alone in the empty pool.

13

Wednesday morning, Willa went to the Bing Society Memorial Museum with the other UDM kids.

The students at Dunwiddle Magic School took this field trip every year. Today, the whole fifth grade was there.

Since the kids in the town's Ordinary School took this field trip every year, too, Willa had been before. How boring. What was the point of seeing the same exhibits, year after year? Couldn't they learn some other history stuff instead?

The museum was located in the house where Zeponiah Bing had lived when she returned to Dunwiddle. Most of the rooms had been kept intact. All the exhibits had the same basic message: Ms. Bing had been a wonderful Flare. There were "before" dioramas and paintings showing the town of Dunwiddle during the Great Frost. There were testimonial letters thanking Bing for saving everyone. There were artifacts of Bing's life. There was a whole room full of stuff about super-strong Flares with the kind of heating magic Bing had, and how amazing they were.

Willa pretty much hated the Bing museum.

As they walked through the first exhibit, Nory linked her arm through Elliott's. "Willa," she called across the room, "will you please take notes for our Gertrude Raspberry project? Since you haven't done anything else?"

Willa sighed and got out her notebook. Nory wasn't being fair. Willa *had* done something else! She had read that whole book and made notes. She knew that fact about Gertrude flunking her polar bear test. And she'd practiced drawing a polar bear.

She just hadn't shown any of it to Nory. Or talked about it. The idea of Nory judging her handwriting and her drawings made her feel seasick. Her parents and teachers already told her she did everything wrong. She didn't need to hear it from Nory, too.

"So this is where Gertrude and Zeppy lived after they saved the town?" Nory asked Ms. Starr.

Zeppy? Willa thought.

"Well, Zeponiah had her teaching job to get back to in Florida," Ms. Starr said. "But when she retired, this is where she and Gertrude chose to settle down, yes."

You could have read that on the sign, Nory, Willa thought. *Only, look. It says Zeponiah, not Zeppy.*

"Write down the years they lived here," Nory instructed Willa. "And describe the wallpaper. Include that it's beginning to peel."

In her notebook, Willa wrote, BLAH BLAH BLAH.

The next room was the oh-so-exciting kitchen (not). On the counters were several oh-so-exciting old-fashioned kitchen utensils (triple not).

Ms. Starr continued to the next room after a quick peek, but Nory lingered. She picked up an egg beater and turned the handle.

"I don't think you're supposed to touch it," Elliott said.

"Yes I am, or they wouldn't leave it out," Nory said. She turned to Willa. "Did you make a list of Zeppy and Gertrude's cooking utensils? And would you describe the pot holder with the polar bear on it?"

"I got it," Willa muttered. In her notes, she wrote, NORY TAKES UP ALL THE AIR IN THE ROOM.

"Did you even *look* at the pot holder?"

"I said I got it!" Willa said. She slashed two lines beneath the word ALL. "I even underlined it, see?! Also, I've been here five million times! The only reason you like Zeponiah's stupid pot holder is because you just moved here!"

Nory stared at her. "If you've been here so many times, why did you act like you didn't know anything about Gertrude Raspberry?"

Willa exploded. "Because I hate how you boss me around!"

She stomped angrily down the hall to catch up with the rest of the school group in Zeponiah Bing's bedroom, which was at the back of the house. She was done talking to Nory Horace. Absolutely done.

But Nory followed her! She caught up to Willa in *ye olde* boring bedroom.

"I have to boss you around because you don't *do* anything!" Nory put her hands on her hips. "You've done zero work, and you have zero ideas! I never wanted to work with you!"

"I didn't want to work with you, either!"

Nory stomped. "At least I tried. At least I worked. You're the worst partner of all time, Willa Ingeborg!"

Tears pricked Willa's eyes. Furious tears.

No, no, no.

She did not want to cry. They were in a historic museum exhibit thingy! If she rained, it would ruin everything!

Could she use Carrot's idea and say *Hello, Furious Tears That Are Totally Nory's Fault. I see you*? Could she acknowledge her feelings without letting them overwhelm her?

No, Willa could not. She was too upset.

A tear rolled down her cheek.

"Really, Willa?" Nory said. *"Really?"*

A raindrop splashed to the floor, leaving a wet spot in the dust.

Within seconds, it was drizzling all over the historic bedroom exhibit.

Drizzling on bedside table stacked with Zeponiah Bing's favorite reading material.

Drizzling over Bing's ancient bathrobe that hung on a hook by the closet door.

Drizzling on Bing's bedside lamp, her historic quilt, the display of embroidered petticoats and pantaloons, and the paintings of her and Gertrude.

"Help!"

"Is it that wonky UDM girl again?"

"Why does she do this?"

"I want my mommy!"

The typical kids from the other classes were freaking out.

Willa gulped as she took in all the chaos.

"I'm freezing!" wailed a girl with sodden curls.

"Stop your stupid rain, Willa!" yelled horrid Lacey Clench.

Willa *would* stop if she could! Didn't the others understand that?

Coach Vitomin hustled a bunch of the the typical fifth graders out of the bedroom. They made sounds of dismay as they scurried down the hall.

"You really must stop, Willa," Ms. Starr told her kindly. "Try your techniques!"

Willa took a deep breath. She tried *so hard* to calm down. But she was still drizzling.

"Should I go outside?" she asked her teacher.

Ms. Starr shook her head. "There are too many rooms between us and the front entrance," she said. "I think you should stay still and try to get calm. That way the rain will only be in this one room." She stood tall and clapped her hands. "All right, UDM students! It'll be raining a little while longer, so help me save the artifacts!" Ms. Starr called. "Andres!" She pointed at the hook. "Get Bing's jacket!"

Andres slipped out of his brickpack and zoomed into the air. He flew across the ceiling until he was near the hook and launched himself at Bing's ancient bathrobe. Protecting it, he zipped out of the room. Ms. Starr told Nory to run after him with the historic quilt. "Now, Marigold—shrink the paintings!" commanded Ms. Starr.

Marigold hurried to the wall of art. She bit her lip and furrowed her brow. *Plip! Plip! Plip!* One by one, she took the heavy paintings off their mounts and shrank them. She handed them to Pepper, who covered them with her jacket and ran them into the next room. Willa guessed someone would find a way to unshrink them later.

Meanwhile, Ms. Starr was yelling, "Elliott! Bing's ye olde petticoats and pantalooons! They're attached to the wall but you can freeze them in a block of ice to preserve the embroidery."

Elliott colored. "But . . ."

"We'll flare-dry them afterward!" Ms. Starr explained. "Save the pantaloons!"

Willa tried to stop raining.

She said hello to the furious rain, but that didn't work.

She tried reciting the poem about the mermaid, but that didn't work.

She tried the hokey breathing exercise, but that didn't work, either.

"And, Bax," Ms. Starr said, turning. "Can you turn into a plastic tarp?"

"No."

"Can you try?"

"Um . . . maybe?" Bax looked nervous.

"You could save the day if you can manage it. Get to it!"

Bax closed his eyes, scrunched his face, and— *sslinkh*. He turned to plastic and fluttered to the ground. He was bright yellow.

"Not a tarp but a poncho!" Ms. Starr cried. "Well done, Bax! Now, Sebastian, lend me a hand!"

Together, Ms. Starr and Sebastian spread Poncho-Bax over the bedside table, protecting Bing's favorite reading material. Willa could tell Ms. Starr was thoughtfully using this crisis as a chance to spur Bax, Elliott, and Marigold into using their talents under pressure. What a great teacher she was!

Nory came back into the room and looked around. She came over to Willa, dripping. "Can't you at least try to stop?" she barked. "We're in a museum!"

"Of course I'm trying to stop!" Willa moaned, beginning to weep. "I've tried like six different techniques!"

"Well, try harder!" said Nory, stamping her feet. "You don't have to be such a crybaby about it! Grow up and stop raining!"

Whoa.

That was it.

The Upside-Down Magic class was supposed to be a team.

That meant, if you were in UDM, you did *not* yell at another UDM kid about having terrible magic in the middle of a big public museum.

You just did not do it. Too many other people mocked the UDM kids all the time. So UDM kids never, ever mocked one another.

Willa looked up at her rain cloud. It was medium-sized and drizzly.

She was *so angry* at Nory.

She shrank her cloud to the size of a cat. Shrank it! And then attached it to Nory. It was the same amount of water, though, just coming from the much smaller cloud. It poured furiously on Nory's head.

Nory slapped at the raindrops, trying to bat them away. "Willa! Stop!"

Willa stood up. "You're right, Nory. I *am* a cry-baby. Let me add that to my notes so that we can include it in our stupid project!"

"Willa?" Ms. Starr said, coming over.

"She's drenching me!" cried Nory.

"But the big drizzle has stopped! Well done, Willa!" Ms. Starr said. "Now can you stop your tiny cloud, please?"

Willa tried. She really did try, even though she didn't want to. But as she'd learned in the pool, it was harder to turn off attached clouds than regular ones.

"She's doing it on purpose!" Nory cried, running around the room.

"No, I'm not!" Willa said. (At least, not anymore.)

"Keep trying," urged Ms. Starr.

Willa did keep trying. But the cloud kept raining on Nory.

Nory glared at Willa. Static electricity seemed to spark in her wet hair. Her body shimmered and—*pop!*

Dritten-Nory roared, and a tongue of fire snaked from her mouth.

Willa's rain quenched the flame.

Dritten-Nory roared louder and flew out of the bedroom exhibit, down the hall, through the kitchen, the dining room, the parlor, the front hall, and out the front door, which was held open by a cringing fifth grader.

The rain cloud followed Dritten-Nory out of the museum and into the open air, where at last it evaporated.

Willa, Pepper, Elliott, Marigold, and Sebastian followed, stepping into the sunshine.

The disaster—well, this particular disaster—was over.

14

On the lawn outside the museum, Nory fluxed back into human form.

So embarrassing! Terrible! And all Willa's fault. Nory fumed as Pepper handed her a stack of paper towels.

Even after Nory was dry, everyone had to wait. Ms. Starr was still indoors, talking with the museum workers. As soon as the teacher stepped out of the building, Nory ran over. Willa followed. Poncho-Bax was folded over Ms. Starr's arm, and Andres was beside her, once again wearing his brickpack.

"May I please switch partners?" Nory asked Ms. Starr in her talking-to-grown-ups voice.

"Yes!" cried Willa. "I can't work with her."

Nory dropped the politeness. She jerked her head at Willa. "*She's* not doing any work!"

"I am so working! *She* changed projects on me!"

"She has no enthusiasm."

"She wants to be the boss of everything."

"I *have* to be the boss. She doesn't have any ideas."

"We *really* need to change partners."

"We *really, really* do."

Ms. Starr shook her head. "Sorry, girls. You're a team. You need to reconcile your differences."

Drat. Drat. Drat.

Nory's energy drained out of her.

Sulking, she boarded the bus that took them back to Dunwiddle Magic School.

She knew that she and Willa needed to finish their project.

She knew she should ask Willa to come home with her that afternoon so they could work on it. It was due on Friday, which was only two days away.

But Nory didn't offer the invitation. She couldn't bear to look at Willa, period.

Nory worked on her own Wednesday night. And Thursday at lunch. She read and read. She wrote and wrote. She finished an entire first draft of the essay that was supposed to accompany their poster. All by herself. She didn't revise it.

At the end of Thursday, she gave it peevishly to Willa. "Type this, please."

Peevishly, Willa typed it overnight.

On Friday morning, Willa pasted their paragraphs onto the poster board and sketched the polar bear.

Nory painted the polar bear.

Willa added more glitter to make it look as if the bear was going through a snowstorm.

It was . . . acceptable. *Just.*

They didn't use more than five sources, because they didn't have time to read all the books Nory had collected. They didn't include photographs. They didn't write much about Gertrude's life back when she was a kid, or after the Great Frost.

They just didn't.

Nory wasn't proud of the project. She felt bummed as she checked out the other Bing Day posters lining the Dunwiddle hallways.

Sebastian and Marigold had scanned and printed many photographs of old-time parades, which they'd colored in by hand. Pepper and Andres's poster on single-sex education had no pictures and only writing. It wasn't entertaining, but they'd typed it single space and with super skinny margins. They would get an O, for sure. Elliott and Bax's poster was titled *Disgusting Foods of 1893* and had menus and detailed drawings of food on toast. Salmon on toast. Oysters on toast. Asparagus on toast. It had clearly taken a lot of research, *and* it was funny.

Plus there were posters from the other fifth-grade classes. A few were half-baked, but most of them were really good.

Nory lifted her chin. She would look on the bright side. Their Gertrude poster wasn't great, but it was done. And this afternoon was the parade. She loved parades!

As soon as the final bell rang, Nory put on her antlers. She'd bought multiple sets from the novelty store in town. She gave a pair to Pepper, who put them on. Andres and Sebastian put theirs on, too. She offered a pair to Bax, and he wrinkled his nose—but he put them on. He hated looking silly, but he cared about the UDM class sticking together.

In the hall, kids milled around by their lockers. Some were going straight to the parade and meeting their parents under the big clock in the town square. Others were going home first to drop off their school stuff.

Nory spotted Willa, Marigold, and Elliott talking. She would be good-spirited and offer antlers to all three of them. After all, she was a nice person and didn't exclude people.

"Antlers?" she said, holding out three sets. "Team UDM!"

Marigold took a pair and put them on.

But Willa plucked them straight off Marigold's head! Refusing to meet Nory's gaze, she said, "Bing Day is not about antlers."

"Oh, *come on*," said Nory. "Antlers are cute! And festive. It's a way to show class spirit!"

"All of us UDM kids are meeting at the big clock," said Elliott. He didn't look at Nory, either. He kicked at the floor with the toe of his sneaker. "We'll be together anyhow."

"Yeah, but with antlers, everyone will *know* we're together," said Nory. She eyeballed Marigold. "You in?"

Marigold shrugged. "I don't know. I agree that they're cute."

"That's because you're not from Dunwiddle!" snapped Willa.

"Actually, I *am* from Dunwiddle now," said Marigold. "I mean, this is where my life is. And Nory's life, too. And Bax's."

"But it's not a silly-hat type of parade!" Willa argued. "It's a ye olde parade to celebrate Zeponiah

Bing. It's historical. If you wear antlers, people will think you're weird."

"So?" Nory said. "Weird is good!"

Color rose in Willa's cheeks. "Not everyone likes looking silly. Antlers make some people feel really awkward, Nory!"

"Take the antlers," Nory said to Elliott.

He tucked his hands into his pockets.

"Seriously?" Nory said. "You're going to let Willa boss you around?"

"Don't let *Nory* boss you around!" Willa cried.

Nory waggled the antlers in Elliott's face. "Take! The adorable! Antlers!"

The air hummed.

Would he or wouldn't he?

"We can't win no matter what we do," Marigold told Elliott.

Elliott nodded. "You're right. But I have an idea." He took hold of Nory's arm with one hand and grabbed Willa with the other.

"Walk," he commanded. "Marigold, you come, too."

What? Was Elliott bossing them around now?

The four of them strode down the hall to the supply closet, a small room filled with brooms, extra light bulbs, pet food for the Fuzzy lab, and cardboard boxes. Sometimes Nory hid out in the supply closet with Pepper. It was tiny, but cozy.

Elliott opened the door. "Nory, Willa, please go in."

"No way. I don't want her in my closet," said Nory, scowling at Willa.

Willa snorted. "It's not your closet. It's the janitor's!"

Elliott groaned. "It's Bing Day. Will you please just go in?"

"I don't see what Bing Day has to do with it," said Nory. But she didn't want to make Elliott even angrier, so she stepped in and turned on the light.

With a dramatic sigh, Willa followed.

Elliott slammed the door on both of them.

What? Nory couldn't believe it. Had Elliott and Marigold *trapped* them in the supply closet? Just the two of them?!

"I'm sick of this war between you two!" yelled Elliott through the door. "Marigold's sick of it, too!"

"Yeah!" yelled Marigold. "You're making things bad for the whole UDM class!"

"Me?" Nory protested. "I *love* our class!"

"You sure don't act like it," Willa snapped.

"You're the one who rained on *me* in the middle of a field trip!" Nory cried. "You're the one who won't show antler spirit!"

"Figure it out, both of you!" yelled Elliott.

"Are you locking us in?!" Nory cried, her voice rising at the end.

"No, the door's not locked, but don't come out until you make up and end your fight. If you can't be friends, figure out how to be *friendly*. Otherwise no one in our class will speak to either of you and you can forget joining us at the parade."

There was the receding sound of footsteps.

"They're gone," Willa said in disbelief.

"They can't be."

"They are." Willa's face crumpled. "I can't believe they shut us in the closet."

Water started pouring from the ceiling.

Not a nice, light drizzle of water.

Not even full-on rainy-day water.

Storm water, cascading down with the force of a raging waterfall.

Not again. "Stop!" Nory cried. "That's a really hard rain!"

Willa's hair was plastered to her face. "I can't believe Marigold and Elliott left us here!" she moaned.

"Well, I'm getting out," Nory said. She turned the slippery door handle—and the knob fell off in her hand.

Oh, no. Nory was horrified. "We're stuck!" She tried to reattach the doorknob but she couldn't. And the door wouldn't open.

The supply closet was filling up alarmingly fast.

Water covered their ankles. Then their knees.

Some water seeped out through the crack beneath the door, but the downpour was so strong that it made little difference.

Nory pounded on the door. She flung her body at it, but it refused to budge.

Soon, both girls had to dog-paddle in order to keep their heads above the rapidly rising water.

We could drown, Nory realized. *We could really and truly drown.*

One glance at Willa told Nory that she was thinking the same thing.

"I would stop if I could," Willa said, lifting her chin and desperately treading water. "I really would! I'm trying all the techniques I know, but nothing's working! Probably because I'm so scared!"

Nory had an idea. She did!

"Don't worry," she told Willa. "One sec!" She screwed shut her eyes.

Squid, squid, squid, she thought. And *Puppy, puppy, puppy! Come on, squippy!*

Her bones rippled. Her flesh bunched up, then stretched apart.

Woof! Squippy-Nory barked. She dove beneath the water, using her strong front puppy legs to swim to the bottom of the room. She wedged one paw into the crack at the bottom of the door to brace herself, then slithered her rear squid tentacles *through* the crack.

Flump, flump! With her longest, stickiest tentacle, she slapped the outside of the supply closet door. She searched and flopped and stretched, until—*YES!* The outside doorknob! She felt it with her tentacle!

With great care, and still holding her breath, Squippy-Nory twisted the doorknob. It clicked open! She retracted her tentacle quickly as the door flew wide. Water cascaded out. Cresting the wave was Willa, waving her arms and kicking.

Floomph. Nory sucked in a big breath of air and fluxed back into her girl body.

The water puddled throughout the hall. Willa landed on the floor as if she'd been dropped.

Willa's rain trickled to a stop. She breathed a sigh of relief.

They were really and truly okay. Willa began to laugh. "Saved by squippy!" she said. "Squippy may not look heroic, but she has tentacles of power!"

Nory laughed, too. "She squiddles on the floor and chews on people's shoes. She climbs up people's legs and squirts squid ink at them! But in a pinch, Squippy-Nory is on your side."

"You held on to your human mind when it counted," Willa told her.

"Yes, I did!" said Nory. "But also, I might have squiddled a little."

"It happens to the best of us," Willa said.

"Squiddle?"

"Out-of-control magic."

Nory sighed and squeezed some water from her hair. "I guess I've been hard on you, huh?"

"Yeah. It just . . ." Willa swallowed. "It just seems like you have everything easy, and still, you pick on me. Like, you're popular. And your magic is fun, with the flying and the Blurper Dragon. You can even do water animals! Plus you play kittenball, and you never seem scared to talk in class, and you always get Os on your math tests. I've seen them. It's like everything at school goes perfectly for you, and then you're mean to me 'cause I'm not as awesome as you or something. It doesn't even make sense."

Nory looked surprised. "Um, hello? Haven't you heard about what I did at the Sage Academy entrance exam? I bit my own father and tried to eat a unicorn. Plus I almost set the place on fire. I don't even get to live with my dad and my siblings anymore. *You* have these smiley parents and fancy art supplies and these lunches that look like they came from a restaurant."

"Any flunking you did was a long time ago," said Willa. "Now you're like super-student! I bet you got all Os."

Nory smiled to herself. "I did get all Os."

"See? I've never, ever gotten an O," Willa said. "Not one. And I can't blame Ms. Starr. I don't finish my homework! I start and do some of it but then . . . I just stop. Or I finish my homework and I don't bring it in. I took notes for our project, you know. And I printed out research from my dad's computer. And I practiced drawing polar bears. I just never showed any of it to you because I thought you'd be all critical."

Nory shook her head. "I thought you weren't doing *anything*."

"I know. I just . . . I felt, like, private about it," Willa said. "With you being so perfect at school and all."

"I don't feel perfect," Nory said. "I just want to do a good job and make my dad proud, so it matters to me." She shrugged. "I've definitely been pushy."

"Just a little," Willa said. She gave Nory a tiny push.

Nory gave Willa a tiny push back, and chuckled.

They sat in the enormous puddle in the hallway, and their chuckling got louder and louder, until the the chuckles became giddy, uncontrollable, we-almost-died-but-then-we-didn't laughter.

Willa felt as if a weight had been lifted from her.

They were all right, the two of them. She and Nory would probably never be best friends, but Willa could tell that the war was over.

"I'm sorry, Nory," she said. "Thanks for saving us."

"You're welcome," said Nory. "And I'm sorry I yelled at you so much."

Willa suddenly wanted Nory's opinion. She bit her lip. "Hey, do you know what Marigold thinks?"

"About what?"

"About me. She thinks I have water magic."

"Huh?"

"She thinks I'm not an Upside-Down Flare at all. And that there might be more than five Fs. She says she has shrinking magic, and that maybe I have water magic." Willa hesitated. "I don't know about Elliott. Maybe he's a double talent? A weak Flare and a strong Freezer? Or maybe Elliott and I are both . . . well . . . Fluids?"

Nory cocked her head.

"Or maybe not," Willa said, worried that bringing up Elliott had hurt their truce.

But Nory nodded. "It makes a lot of sense!"

"It does?"

"My father wouldn't like it, but I think it's possible. I mean, maybe magic is more complicated than the five Fs."

Willa nodded. "Yeah, I think it is."

Nory stood up. "Let's change into dry clothes. The parade's about to start."

Willa stood, too. She spotted Nory's wet and droopy antlers, which were lying in the enormous puddle. "Let's dry these off with the hand dryer in the bathroom. The ones in your bag, too."

Nory grinned. "You mean you'll wear them? For real?"

"For real," said Willa. "You were right. The UDM class should stick together."

15

The center of town was crowded, but Nory knew where to go. She took hold of Willa's backpack strap and pulled her toward the Upside-Down Magic crew.

"Wowzers," Nory said as they slipped in by the others. She took in all the people, and her mouth fell open. So many people! So many flags and pennants! So many historical costumes! "People really go all out, don't they?"

Marigold saw her and smiled. "It's Dunwiddle!" she exclaimed. "Of course we do!"

Nory handed out antlers to those who didn't have them yet. Willa adjusted hers more snugly behind her ears.

"Does this mean everything's good?" Elliott asked.

Nory linked her arm through Willa's. "Everything's good."

"I hope it's not going to rain," Marigold said, looking at the darkening sky.

"Of course it isn't," Elliott said. "It never rains on Bing Day!"

Still, Nory felt a flutter of unease as she looked at the weather. The clouds were dark gray—no, they were almost black. She shivered and buttoned her coat.

"The parade is starting!" Bax cried.

First came the marching band. They played trumpets, trombones, and low burping tubas. The band members were dressed in ye olde costumes of 1893, complete with tassels, epaulets, and conical hats.

Next came a float showing landmarks of the town of Dunwiddle.

Then the mayor drove by in an old-fashioned black car with round headlights.

Then a bunch of other old people, driving more old-fashioned cars.

Then some bagpipers in kilts. Why? Nory didn't know.

Then came a troupe of folk dancers wearing clogs and sashes. Then a float that showed the town of Dunwiddle buried in snow.

This parade was nothing like the summer parades back in Nutmeg, where Nory used to live. But Nory loved it anyway.

Andres floated above the others like a balloon, his leash gripped tightly by his sister, Carmen. Aunt Margo and several other Flyers watched the parade from high up. Elliott's dad had Elliott's little brother on his shoulders. Pepper's brothers were jumping and clapping. Bax's mom was there. Marigold's grandparents watched from a bench several yards back, and so did Sebastian's family.

Willa's family showed up a little later—the Ingeborg parents plus a tall blond girl Nory figured must be Willa's sister, Edith. They smiled their chilly Ingeborg smiles.

Suddenly the parade stopped. Willa nudged Nory. "They're pausing. That means it's time for the Bing Day Sing-Along."

All at once, the marching band, the bagpipers, and the tambourine players began to play the same tune. It was jolly music. The whole town launched into song:

Oh, Bing, Dunwiddle loves you so!
Your sunshine power melted snow!
Clap your hands and loudly sing!
Clap your hands, now clap for Bing!

They all clapped in a rhythm. Clap clap clap clap clap clap CLAP!

Oh, Bing, Dunwiddle loves you so!
Your sunshine power melted snow!

Stomp your feet and loudly sing!
Stomp your feet, now stomp for Bing!

They all stomped in the same rhythm. Stomp stomp stomp stomp stomp stomp STOMP! It was pretty cool, a whole town singing together. Nory and Willa grinned at each other.

Oh, Bing, Dunwiddle loves you so!
Your sunshine power melted snow!
Snap your fingers, loudly sing!
Snap your—

The gray sky opened with a crash.

Lighting cracked.

Rain poured down.

So. Much. Rain.

No one had umbrellas, not even the UDM kids. After all, Willa didn't rain outdoors, and it never, ever rained on Bing Day. That meant that all of the people who believed Zeponiah Bing's enormous Flare power kept her holiday sunny—they were wrong! It was *definitely* raining.

The ye olde marching band stopped playing. The bagpipers ran into one another. The tambourine players ran into the bagpipers.

The cloggers looked sad. A toddler started weeping, and two more joined in. Here and there, Flares with heating magic made warm spots for people to huddle in, but everyone was still outrageously wet.

"Kids, we might have to run for cover," Ms. Starr said.

Oh, no! Nory didn't want to leave. It was her first Bing Day Parade!

"Can't somebody stop it?" asked Marigold.

She looked at Willa.

Sebastian looked at Willa.

One by one, Nory saw *all* the UDM kids turn to look at Willa.

"*I* didn't make it rain!" Willa exclaimed.

"We know! But, Willa—you can *stop* it!" Nory said.

But Willa shook her head. Ms. Ingeborg shook *her* head. Mr. Ingeborg shook *his* head. Willa's sister, Edith, said, "Willa's magic doesn't work that way. You guys should know that already, if you're in her class. She can't stop big rains. Not even when she starts them."

But Willa *had* shrunk that large drizzling cloud in the museum down to a small and furiously raining one, and she *had* attached the small and furiously raining one to Nory. Could she do something like that here? Nory turned to her friend. "Willa, you *can* help!"

"Me?" Willa squeaked. "No! I can only make it rain indoors!"

"But you don't have to *make* it rain. Or even *stop* it from raining. You just need to *move* the rain! Or shrink the cloud?"

"Yeah," Elliott chimed in, understanding. "Attach it to something, like you did when you made the cloud follow me at the pool!"

"And me at the museum!" Nory said.

Willa took a step backward. "I can't attach a giant cloud I didn't make. I can only attach a tiny cloud that I made myself!"

Nory stepped toward her and touched Willa's arm. "Try, Willa? Please?"

"Please?" echoed Elliott.

Nory had faith. "You can do it, Willa," she said. "I know you can!"

Willa gulped. Everyone in the UDM class was looking at her. Nory, Marigold, Elliott . . . everyone!

They all wanted her to do something she couldn't do.

There was no way she could attach a giant rain cloud to something moving.

And it wasn't just one cloud. It was many clouds clustered together.

And there wasn't anything to attach them to, anyway!

Willa looked at her classmates. A small voice bubbled up within her. *Breathe*, the voice said. *Your friends believe in you.*

"Come on, Willa!" said Nory. "Try it! It's okay if you don't succeed. But *try*."

Willa closed her eyes and tilted her face to the sky. She searched for the water power inside her.

She looked for the water inside her with love, instead of frustration or anger. She felt love for her classmates, for the parade, for the town of Dunwiddle. Her love for ye olde life itself, which sometimes was stormy—but today seemed shiny and beautiful.

She found the magic in her and she connected her water magic to the water in the sky. She imagined a great finger gently pushing the storm clouds aside.

Just scooch over that way, please, she told the clouds. *Rain on the high school, rain on the park, but right here on Main Street, we're celebrating sunshine, okay? I'm just going to coax you gently over to the side.*

Gasps peppered the air around her, then rippled out farther within the crowd.

Willa felt the caress of sunlight on her face, buttery and warm.

The rain clouds hadn't disappeared, but they'd moved over, just where Willa had pushed them. Now, instead of raining on the entire town, the clouds left Main Street alone. The parade zone was dry.

Pale yellow sunlight shone on the marching band, the cloggers, and the floats. It shone on the crying toddlers, and their wails dried up. It shone on the gleaming tubas, and the tuba players once again belted out their jolly song.

The other musicians picked up the tune. The cloggers resumed clogging. The mayor took off his bowler hat and waved it through the air.

"Onward!" he cried.

The crowd erupted in hoots and hollers and wild applause. Willa felt cool fingers find her hand. It was her mother.

"*You* did that," she told Willa, amazed. "Sweetie, you moved the rain."

"Now you won't have to live in the shed," said Edith. "Next time you rain in the house, you can move it to the bathroom or something."

"She was never going to live in the shed," said Mr. Ingeborg. "Edith, behave."

"That was pretty cool, actually," said Edith, ruffling Willa's wet hair. "I've got to give you credit."

"Three cheers for Willa!" yelled the UDM kids. "Hip hip hooray!"

"Well done, Willa!" Ms. Starr exclaimed. "That was some extraordinary upside-down magic."

"Actually, I don't think it *was* upside-down magic." Willa spoke loudly, and her parents and Ms. Starr leaned in to listen. "Marigold made me do some thinking . . . and Ms. Cruciferous made me think more."

"Think what?" asked Willa's mother.

"I don't think I'm upside down, exactly."

"You don't?" said Ms. Starr.

"No."

"Why not?"

"I don't flare. Not ever."

"That's true," said Willa's mother. "She never does."

"So I think I have some kind of water magic, not

upside-down flaring," said Willa. "Like, a different category. Maybe we could call me a . . . Fluid!"

"Ooooh, that's way better than Fishie," Marigold said.

"What do you think, Ms. Starr?" Willa asked.

Ms. Starr gave a bright smile. "I think it's absolutely possible! There's so much about magic that doesn't fit our five F categories. And you definitely have a right to call your magic a name that feels true for you. We can all respect that in the future."

"Hooray!" Nory cried.

Marigold hugged Willa. "I'm so proud of you."

Willa's mom hugged her, too. "There's a lot going on in your head, little missy," she said. "So much to talk about when we get home."

"Hey, Elliott," said Nory. "Did you see how I helped Willa to realize she could save the parade? I was the one who told Willa to do it! Did you hear me?"

"Yeah," said Elliott. "I did, actually. You were really encouraging."

"I helped Willa do amazing Fluid magic!" Nory continued. "And do you know what that makes me?"

"No." Elliott looked puzzled.

"Gertrude Raspberry!"

Pepper nodded. "Yeah, I can see that!"

"Gertrude was the unsung humble hero who saved Dunwiddle! Just like me!" said Nory.

Willa laughed. "How can you be the unsung humble hero if you tell everyone you're unsung and humble?"

Nory stopped for a minute. "Okay, fine. Good point." Then she smiled. "Willa, *you* saved Bing Day. Willa saved Bing Day!"

Willa glowed. She *had* saved Bing Day. All of these townspeople were clogging and bagpiping right this very second because she had moved the rain. Without her, Willa Ingeborg with the Fluid magic, everyone would have gone home, soaked and sad.

Willa put her arm around Nory. "Thanks for the encouragement, Gertrude."

Nory winked. "Anytime, Zeppy."

16

The next Monday, after the last bell, Nory skipped along with the rest of the UDM kids to the high school pool. Ms. Starr had arranged a celebration.

True, the day had started with a bit of a bummer. The UDM students had all received their grades on the Bing Day projects and Ms. Starr had given Nory and Willa a Q for *Quite good, but nothing to bang a drum about.*

It wasn't a grade worth calling Father about.

In fact, it was a grade to avoid telling Father about.

But truthfully, Nory hadn't been surprised at the grade. They had deserved that Q. On the bright side, Nory *had* learned a lot about Gertrude. And some stuff about teamwork, too. Mostly, she'd learned a lot about Willa.

But other than getting that Q, the day had been awesome. After lunch, a package had been delivered to Ms. Starr. The Bing Society had mailed the UDM class a box of white chocolate polar bears with marshmallow filling. Polar-Bear-Gertrude candies! Ten bears: one for each kid, one for Ms. Starr, and one for Carrot. It was a thank-you treat in honor of Willa, for saving the parade. And to thank the UDM kids for helping save the museum from rainy ruin, even though it was their fault the museum had to be saved in the first place.

Now Nory was hopped up on sugar. She'd be the first kid in the water!

She cannonballed into the deep end.

"Jump in!" Ms. Starr encouraged the others, waving them toward the pool. Their teacher wore an electric-yellow bathing suit with black stripes. It made her look like a joyful bumblebee.

Elliott dove into the deep end with Nory. Willa followed, and Nory didn't even feel jealous when Willa popped up and gave Elliott a splashy high five. She figured she'd join them eventually, but first she swam to the shallow end, where Marigold and Pepper were using the stairs to get into the pool. "Come on in," Nory told them. "It's warm once you get used to it."

Bax got in but refused to use the unicorn floatie, even though it had been repaired with duct tape. Instead, he stayed in the shallow end and held on to the wall. Andres wore his brickpack and stayed in the shallow end, too. He and Bax started a splash war. Coach and Ms. C sat on the edge of the pool.

Sebastian joined Elliott and Willa at the deep end, wearing large flippers and holding on to a foam noodle.

Nory dove beneath the water and popped up again. This was the best way ever to celebrate Willa's amazing Bing Day accomplishment!

Nory found Ms. Starr. "Can I flux? Pleasie please please?"

Ms. Starr glanced at Coach, who glanced at Ms. C.

"Young lady," said Ms. C, folding her arms over her chest, "I do not want to see that porcuphin in my pool ever again."

"No porcuphin!" said Nory. "I promise."

"Keep it small. And nothing with fur. Good gracious. You have no idea how many hair balls I had to pull from the drain after your squitten."

Hair balls? Gross. "Okay, nothing with fur," Nory agreed.

"Do you think you can do pure squid?" Coach asked.

Nory shook her head. "I think my squid will go furry."

"Hey, Nory!" Willa called. "Can you flux into a puffer fish?"

"Do it!" called Elliott.

"Or don't," Bax groused. He sighed. "And if you must, don't you dare poke me."

Silly Bax. Nory wouldn't poke anybody! And puffer fish were nice and small.

But *could* she do puffer fish?

Could she do *any* fish without adding fur? Or growing huge?

"I think you might have puffer fish in you," said Coach encouragingly. "Because of the porcuphin. You know, spiny water creatures are a very specific kind of fluxing. People who do narwhals, for example, can do cowfish, puffer fish, and occasionally even sea urchins."

He gave Nory some reminders about holding on to the human mind plus some fish-fluxing hints he'd read up on since their awkward lesson in the pool.

Nory listened carefully. Then she shook out her limbs. She swooshed her hips. She did a flip in the water. *Bulge, fwoomph, pop!*

"She did it!" Willa cried. "Look, everybody! Nory's a puffer fish!"

Puffer-Fish-Nory waggled her fins. She could breathe in the water! She zipped around in circles and then flung herself into the air, flapping her tiny side fins wildly. Briefly, she saw her reflection in the water.

She looked like a soccer ball, but blue.

She landed in the water and went under again. She sucked in a mouthful of water and popped her face out to spray it all over Bax.

"Aaaaaah!" he cried, trying to splash her back—but Puffer-Fish-Nory was already underwater again. A sea of tiny bubbles gurgled out behind her. She flapped her fins and launched herself across the pool,

popping out of the water and skipping over the surface like a well-thrown stone.

She shot high into the air—*whoop!* Then landed smack in Willa's outstretched arms. *Ploomp!* Like a balloon!

Willa lifted Puffer-Fish-Nory over her head and tossed her to Elliott. "Hey, Elliott, catch!"

Puffer-Fish-Nory landed in Elliott's arms. She squirmed underwater for a quick breath before Elliott tossed her back to Willa. Pepper swam over to join the game. So did Sebastian. Bax paddled his floatie closer.

"I'm open!" he called, lifting his hands. "Throw her here!"

Again and again, Puffer-Fish-Nory soared through the air, dunking underwater every so often to catch a quick breath.

"Hey, Bax, can you do volleyball net yet?" Elliott asked.

"No."

"Well, maybe one day."

"Not if I can help it," Bax said. "Sheesh."

But Puffer-Fish-Nory thought maybe Bax *would* want to someday.

And she thought maybe, someday, Willa would rain outdoors.

And maybe she, Nory, would flux into a whale.

Or a kitten-whale. A kale!

Or even a mermaid. Anything was possible.

Nory, Marigold, and friends return for another

upside-down adventure in:

UPSIDE★DOWN MAGIC #6: THE BIG SHRINK!

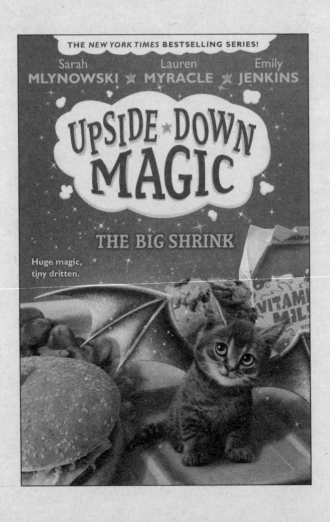

Acknowledgments

Gratitude and magical snowstorms to the team at Scholastic, including but not limited to: David Levithan, Rachel Feld, Maya Marlette, Charisse Meloto, Monica Palenzuela, Lauren Donovan, Tracy van Straaten, Lisa Bourne, Sue Flynn, Melissa Schirmer, Emily Heddleson, Robin Hoffman, Lizette Serrano, and Aimee Friedman. Bags of choco fire trucks and a ye olde clogging dance to Laura Dail, Tamar Rydzinski, Barry Goldblatt, Tricia Ready, Elizabeth Kaplan, Lauren Kisilevsky, Eddie Gamarra, Lauren Walters, and Deb Shapiro. Old-time embroidered pantaloons to Bob, with thanks for all the support. We are grateful to our families: Randy, Al, Jamie, Maya, Mirabelle, Alisha, Daniel, Ivy, Hazel, Todd, Chloe, and Anabelle. Unicorn floaties for all of you! Finally, thanks to our readers. We know you have magic inside of you. And *you* get to decide what to name it.

About the Authors

SARAH MLYNOWSKI is the author of many books for tweens, teens, and adults, including the *New York Times* bestselling Whatever After series, the Magic in Manhattan series, and *Gimme a Call*. She is also the co-creator of the traveling middle-grade book festival OMGBookfest. She would like to be a Flicker so she could make the mess in her room invisible. Visit her online at sarahm.com.

LAUREN MYRACLE is the *New York Times* best-selling author of many books for young readers, including the Winnie Years series, the Flower Power series, and the Life of Ty series. *The Backward Season* is the most recent book in her Wishing Day trilogy. She would like to be a Fuzzy so she could talk to unicorns and feed them berries. You can find Lauren online at laurenmyracle.com.

EMILY JENKINS is the author of many chapter books, including *Brave Red, Smart Frog*, the Toys Trilogy (which begins with *Toys Go Out*), and the Invisible Inkling series. Her picture books include *All-of-a-Kind Family Hanukkah, A Greyhound, A Groundhog, Princessland, Lemonade in Winter,* and *Toys Meet Snow*. She would like to be a Flare and work as a pastry chef. Visit Emily at emilyjenkins.com.